"HELP ME WITH THIS. YOU HAVE NO OTHER CHANCE OF MAKING IT OUT ALIVE...."

"What are you mixing me up in?" I said. "A power play? I won't work blind."

"You don't have any choice," my captor said. "Look, I didn't plan to do it this way, but you felt how badly the ground moved. If Uldhaar doesn't step down, the whole planet is going to go."

"The shaking ground. Uldhaar's doing that?"

"No. But he's keeping me from stopping it before it's too late."

"The earth moved," I said. "From the way you talk it's not a natural phenomenon. What is it? A leftover war weapon? We were a survival training station. We had no weapons development units aboard."

"No," he said, not looking at me. "Not a war weapon. More a tool."

"Not good enough," I said. "What is it?"

"It was supposed to be the ultimate answer to the problem of wartime matériel and supply, but as you can see, the side effect isn't what they expected. And if you don't help me, it's going to rip apart the whole planet...."

THE ICE BEAST

FRANK JAVOR

DAW BOOKS, INC.
DONALD A. WOLLHEIM, PUBLISHER

375 Hudson Street, New York, NY 10014

First Printing, September 1990
1 2 3 4 5 6 7 8 9
PRINTED IN THE U.S.A.

Prologue

The cavern was enormous, walls of ice rising to curve and meet high overhead in cathedrallike arches through which the light of *Thul*'s puny sun filtered feebly. At the center, a platform of battered wood glazed with the cold. Shoulder high, it had more the look of a performer's stage than of a regal dais.

The shouts of a thousand throats were at once a flood and an echo in my ears, stirring the air that reeked of rancid fat and the sharp iron stench of chilling sweat. A thousand throats shouting my fate and I, spread-eagled and stripped to my skin, atop the platform in a vat slowly filling with water steaming not with heat but in contrast to the numbing cold of the air. I did not know the language of my thousand judges, could not grasp their verdict, but I knew that when the water reached me it would, in this frigid temperature, drain from me my body heat and I would slowly and surely die.

Cold. The numbing cold. Relax . . . relax . . . relax! You have experienced the cold of this planet before and you survived it. You have nothing to fear from it now. Relax. . . .

I pushed aside the thought that my previous exposure to *Thul's* open air in anything less than my parka was the dash in my skivvies across the company street from the shower hut to my barracks.

It had been a tradeoff. Stay in the hut to put on some clothes in air choking cold with the spray's humidity, or dash across the company street, slipping on the ice in your clogs, to the relative warmth of your barracks where at least you couldn't see the steam coming off your body as you tried to control its shivering.

A man, short like the others, but looking to be of somewhat slighter build under his layers of skins and bindings, poked at my ribs with a blunt stick I'd seen him twirl on his fingers like a small baton. A juggler of sorts, I took him to be. Perhaps the court jester, if they had such in this ice-cavern-dwelling tribe I was sure was howling for my destruction.

If his poking was meant to get my attention, it succeeded. I moved my mind from the warm glow in which it was keeping me enveloped against the relentless cold to focus on his face grinning down at me over the rim of the slowly filling tub.

I heard him speak, laughing as he did so, not to me, but to the other man on the platform beside him. Taller than the one I took to be the jester, I remembered the two swords he had thrust through his belt though I could not see them over the rim of the vat that held me prisoner. Both blades unusual in their length so that I guessed my captors to be aware of the shortness of their reach in combat.

The Jester turned from Two-Swords to the crowd, shouting to them above their din, his hands waving, coming together, one wrapped around the other.

The crowd roared its approval. Two-Swords stared at the Jester. Stared at him long. He did not smile, but at last he nodded his head and the roar of the crowd redoubled. Laughter and loud shouts. I sensed I'd witnessed a clash of wills.

I felt the bonds on my wrists and ankles being slashed free and myself lifted out of the slowly filling vat and set upright on my feet.

Shoulders and bodies and grunts and the vat was pushed aside and I stood atop the small square of the raised dais, alone except for Two-Swords, now sitting on a small drum set at one corner of the platform. The Jester had dropped to sit cross-legged on its floor at the corner opposite him.

I could sense anticipation in the crowd surging closer, read it in their faces upturned to the cold light filtering down from the vaulted ice ceiling. Saw eagerness in their eyes and in their grins. And when I saw the man being thrust forward from their midst, I knew what the Jester had in mind for me.

Voices. I heard new voices entering. Women's and here and there the piping shriek of a child. This was no longer a gathering of peers to judge my fate, it had become a spectacle pure and simple, to be enjoyed by all. And I, my fate, was the main, the only attraction.

I stared at the Jester looking at me, his grin unreadable.

But their champion had leaped to the dais, leaped without using his hands and from a standing start, and I felt a certain dismay at this display of his physical strength. They were small men all, my captors, barely reaching the level of my chest. He was even shorter, barrel-stomached and thicker through the chest than I had ever been. And heavier than my two hundred by another thirty pounds at least. At six-four I had the reach on him, but that was all I had. There was no way I was going to take him in any kind of primitive grappling and, from the yellow-toothed grin splitting his face, he knew it.

I looked about me at the mass of the mob pressing close. From their faces and nudgings, they knew it, too.

The tribal champion showed me his teeth and began stripping away the outer layers of his clothing until he was left with a single kiltlike rag hung loosely about his hips to match my nakedness.

He stamped both his feet, planted them firmly, and held out his thick arms to me, the fingertips gesturing me closer. It was plain he meant to have some sport with me before he got down to the serious business of proving, on my body, how guilty I was of my accused crime; how unworthy of any consideration of mercy.

The crowd roared its approval. From somewhere among them I heard a woman scream, a feral sound, and I did not need the cold to feel the hair rise up on my neck and along my spine. Blood. They sensed blood, my blood, and I felt their circled mass surge even closer.

I looked out over them. I looked at the Jester grinning. Even Two-Swords, seated atop his drum, the loser in the test of wills I felt I'd witnessed, even he was grinning.

Last of all, I looked at their tribal champion grinning at me all the way to his yellow back teeth. No one had told me the meaning of this confrontation. I did not understand their language to gather it for myself.

But I knew a blood crowd when I smelled one. I'd come to *Thul* on the rumored track of a phenomenally swift racing animal and here I was standing naked with the feral stink of a blood crowd filling my nostrils and choking in my throat, my life on the line again. *How? How do I get myself into these things? How, dammit, how?*

CHAPTER 1

I took a last deep breath of the shuttle's warm cabin air and held it. I was remembering my first experience with *Thul*'s punishing cold. My gasp of surprise and the knifing pain in my chest when, stepping off the gig bringing me aboard the then SpaceNav station, I'd drawn my first unsuspecting breath of the ice world's sinus-numbing air.

"Let's go," I heard from behind me. The shuttle's only other passenger, a rumpled-looking, well-fleshed man who hadn't troubled to hide his impatience the whole of our long trip in, was pressing me closely. I ducked my head and stepped out onto the frozen, iron-hard earth of *Thul*.

I stepped out, the wind catching me not altogether by surprise. Out of sight below the horizon were the craggy mountain peaks amongst which the outlying survival training camps had once been scattered. One sharp tower of ice was scarred deep in my memory.

But here at the incoming pad the vista was of ice open to a sky drained of color by the debilitating cold; open to a wind which varied only in intensity, never in frequency. It blew, always.

I exhaled slowly, inhaled as cautiously. *Thul* wasn't the way I remembered it from my SpaceNav days, but it didn't have the abandoned look I'd expected of it either. The rows of barracks were gone, but that they had been cleared away completely and not just abandoned to the wind was unexpected. As were the coils of sharp wire I saw circling the squat operations tower at one end of the pad.

I felt a slap on my shoulder and turned to face a thickset man with a full beard studded with his frozen breath. He was wearing the patch of a civilian penal guard on his blue-and-orange checkered parka.

A civilian guard on *Thul* . . . and checking incoming passengers? That was a surprise. It showed in my face.

He laughed, a short, unpleasant sound. "You been here before." It was not a question, he was stating a fact.

I nodded. "Second Police Action," I said. "I was stationed here."

"You came back?" He didn't say it, but the "why would anybody want to?" was plain in his voice and I understood his point.

But this was no nostalgia trip for me. I was

here because Harry Judd, a former shipmate who'd been too clever for his own good and ended up dead, had touted me into believing him when he said that somewhere on this frozen ball of ice there was a living something that could outrun, outswim, and outfly anything else alive.

Aside from the fascination with anything that could be raced that I suppose Harry had a right to expect of me, there was my curiosity as to what such a triple-talented entity might look like.

Curiosity and the hope that, if it existed and I found it, I could work up a piece for which the networks or the syndicates or even a private house might pay me enough to let me keep free-lancing the galaxies with my camera while I sorted things out now that the SpaceNav had decided that it could survive without my services as a Photo Mate Second and had handed me a "battlestar" discharge.

But even if Harry hadn't warned me that those who'd bred the rumored racing phenomenon were at great pains to keep secret its existence until they were ready to spring it on their intergalactic gaming brethren, I still wouldn't have gone about blatting to a penal guard my reason for coming aboard even if he'd looked to be interested. This one didn't.

That suited me. The last thing I wanted anyone on *Thul* to suspect at this point was that a working photographer had come aboard to root out their particular secret and photograph it if he could.

The guard was pointing at my camera case with a mittened hand. "You got a license for that?"

"Yes," I said. "You want to see it?"

Police action restrictions on cameras and other communications equipment to civilians and service personnel alike were still in place, and Bureau licenses like mine were a rarity.

"No, not me. Later maybe."

He turned to my fellow passenger, who was standing fidgeting beside the small command skimmer into which someone had already dumped my one parachute bag. The man seemed to be traveling with but the one bag over his shoulder. That marked him for me as either a knowledgeable traveler or a man in too much of a hurry to pack. Except for my camera case, I carried but the single parachute bag that I'd salvaged so far back that I no longer remembered when or where. It might even have been here on *Thul.*

I settled my camera case in the rear of the skimmer and climbed into a front seat. My impatient co-passenger started to lift up a thick-fingered hand as I did so. Maybe that was where he wanted to sit.

But that was his problem not mine, and in a moment, he squeezed into the narrow back seat and the stocky guard was beside me and firing up.

The commander who'd set up the station didn't like the snarls and the whines of landings and takeoffs so he'd located his administration complex at a decent distance from the racket and hassle and I expected that was where we were headed now.

We were up and passing the operations tower and its protective fencing of coiled wire. I nodded at it. "Ah, the natives are getting restless, I see."

It was a semi-joke and a carryover from my station days and maybe not all that funny. *Thul* had its natives, but like Earthside's Bigfoot, while there was plenty of sign, I don't recall anyone ever catching more than a distant glimpse of any.

Or maybe the guard was staring at me because all us SpaceNav types were long ago shipped out and nobody now aboard the planet paid much attention to the booming sounds that could be heard coming from the mountains below the horizon from time to time.

Avalanches and the glacial ice cracking with the bitter cold were the cause, we'd finally decided. But "the natives are restless" got to be a tag line for almost anything that struck us as even marginally odd and, passing what looked to be a barricaded tower, I said it now, more from force of returning habit than from any sense that it might have made. That and to perhaps invite an explanation.

The guard turned his eyes back to his guiding of the skimmer. He shrugged. "The natives are always restless," he said. So maybe he did know the tag line . . . or the natives *were* becoming restless.

The old man behind the spacepad hostel counter needed a shave. "You can take a shot at finding a room in town," he said, "but it'll cost you an arm and a leg and you're lucky if what they stuff the sack with that they give you to sleep on don't walk away with you in the night."

"I know the place," I said and let it go at that.

He gave me the same "then why would you want to come back?" look I'd gotten from the guard and pulled back the room key he'd been pushing toward me with a grimy forefinger.

I did know the place. I also knew that if I meant to track down a potential action animal, my best chance wasn't likely to be where the peace officer uniforms were wall to wall.

"What can I rent in the way of transport?" I asked the old man.

He wasn't wasting any amenities on me. He waved a disinterested hand at the uniforms. "Nothing," he said. "They already got anything bigger than a skimdisk."

A skimdisk. I remembered an open platform barely big enough for one man to stand on that rode a downward blast of air. The only protection from the sweep of the biting wind a man-high clear shield that went halfway around its rim and could be slid down to half that height when wanted. If it was salvage from my former station, it would also have two sets of controls. One at the normal waist level, the other on the floor to be operated from a crouched position. There were times when to stand tall had not been the best of ideas.

"A skimdisk's okay," I said. It wasn't my choice for comfort, but it would have to do.

The old man laughed. His stainless steel teeth were a lousy fit. "You want to kill yourself riding one of those dishpans? You know how tricky they are to handle?"

I was getting a little tired of looking at him. "Would it ease your mind any if I told you I was stationed here during the peace action and rode them all the time?"

He rolled yellow eyeballs. "Another one," he said and took down a key from the near-empty board behind him. He held it out to me with a gesture to one side. "Out that door, turn left. There's a shed at the end of the lot. Two skimdisks in there. Take your pick, key fits both."

"Want me to sign anything?" I said.

"No, you ain't going anywhere without checking through here first. I'll catch you with the bill then."

No signature, no record. I understood the old man's grift. Picayune, but what else was there for him on *Thul*?

His rolled eyeball bit hadn't escaped me. "Another one?" I said. "Another one who?" But all the answer I got was a shrug and an, "Anything else?"

It was my turn to shrug. I jerked a thumb at the uniforms milling around behind me. I was curious about them, too. What struck me was that they were not service people, but peace officers. "What's with all the civilians?" I said. "You got a convention going or something?"

"A convention? On this lump of ice?" But he didn't answer that question either.

I took the skimdisk key the old man was holding out to me from his bony fingers, picked up my para bag, gave my camera case strap a hitch over my shoulder and went on out the door he'd indicated.

On the top of my balding head, down toward the front, I have a souvenir of the late peace action that the field medic lieutenant had done a better than great job of sewing up. You can hardly see the scar unless you get the light across it just right.

But just because you can't see it doesn't mean that I don't know it's there. I know because it has a way of reminding me whenever it feels I am about to get myself into something excessivly stupid.

I didn't see that asking about uniforms, civilian or military, was excessively anything. So why then was the souvenir on my head sending me the urge to reach up and scratch?

I fired up the nearest of the two skimdisks. The other sat back against the wall and had not been used since someone skidded it to a stop long enough ago for the marks on the frozen earth floor to have picked up their own accumulation of debris. These dishpans, as the old man had called them, were rugged, but they were sensitive to body balance and learning to ride one took its measure of dues in lumps and bruises and an occasional broken bone.

I swung my camera case around in front of me, straddled my para bag, which I'd centered on the platform between my feet, and nudged the lift bar with the edge of my fist.

The skimdisk started to rattle and bounce, the rim striking here and there like the thrown top of a storage jar.

I nudged the lift bar a little farther and the jarring stopped, becoming instead a kind of unsettling circular swirl.

I leaned my body to one side and had the satisfaction of feeling the disk start a small sweep away from the direction of my tilting. Fine, my body had not lost the knack, its muscle memory remembering.

I let the curving sweep carry me out the shed doorway. In the clear, I straightened my course, hit the power button and felt the momentary dip and rise as the supporting column altered strength and direction to drive the disk forward.

I'd forgotten how noisy a skimdisk was until I saw the startled faces turning toward me. A skimdisk is not a smooth ride, but it can be an exhilarating one and I'd forgotten that, too.

Now I rocked my body from side to side, enjoying the swell and fall of its power roar; enjoying the clouds of shards and debris swirling up on either side as the stream of supporting air escaped its confining apron first on one side and then on the other.

The sound had brought the old man out

from behind his counter to lean half out his open door his yellow eyes wide. I waved an arm at him as I swept past. A skimdisk is a tricky thing to ride and I rode this one well. His open-mouthed stare more than made up for any slight I might have felt at his offhand manner with me.

But I kept up the foolishness only a moment longer. Attention was not what I wanted, or needed, just now. I knew well enough where *Thul*'s town area was and now I straightened my course and headed directly for it across the open ice. It had to be my imagination, but I thought I saw a head rise up from behind a frozen hillock around a bend in the road I'd just left and look fixedly after me.

CHAPTER 2

I topped the high rim of ice and careened down the slope of the dishlike hollow in which the shabby buildings along Heyday's one main street huddled out of the wind whipping past overhead. Never more than a way station on the way to a roaring drunk for the station personnel, the town had no reason to exist once we were gone and it looked it. Here were the fallen-in roofs and the staring, smashed windows I'd expected to see when I stepped off the shuttle at the incoming pad. Nobody was in sight along the broken street, which made sense to me.

I eased my skimdisk to a stop in front of a two-storied building smaller than the others. It was one which I remembered as not being overly hostile to my former SpaceNav rate.

Photographers were, and probably still are, looked upon as borderline head cases, and maybe that's what it takes to be a good one. I wouldn't care to speculate.

Or maybe it was our rating badge, the so-called crow, we each wore on our left sleeve. It depicted an early camera. A folding, bellowed box that in outline did have something of the shape of a coffin. So obviously the coffin rate was what we were called, and maybe it was that that gave some of us strange ideas. I do know that if a ship made it back from a mission and we saw a single stretcher being lifted out by the medics, we could make book that it was the photographer aboard who was strapped in it.

I pocketed the key, stepped off the disk, gathered up my para bag, and crossed to the sagging twin doors. There were no sidewalks in Heyday. They weren't needed, not with ground that stayed frozen as hard as any concrete the year round.

Inside, there was no more heat than there needed to be. No lobby in this place. Just the open dining room with a few rough tables at which a scant half dozen men sat eating. Three at one table, the others scattered. No women that I could see and that was no surprise. Nobody would bring his family to a frozen outpost like *Thul*, during the peace action, and the women who'd been here then were long gone with its closing.

At one side was a narrow desk with a cash register on it and another old man behind it. He had less hair than I remembered, and he could have been the twin of the one who'd told me the town would be full up. I put my para bag down on the scuffed and dented floor and pulled what I took to be the register toward me. I used my own pen to sign in, flashed my I.D. for verification. I didn't need to ask if they had a room. They had nothing else but.

"What's on the menu?" I asked.

The old man didn't blink. "Specialty of the house," he said.

"Stew will be fine," I said. "So long as there's enough of it."

I am six four, and Earthside I do weigh two hundred. Whenever I ate off the base, I would have to ask for two orders if I didn't want to get up hungry.

The old man was looking at me. "I remember you," he said. He glanced at my left sleeve. "You used to order double of everything."

And again I was treated to a "what are you doing back?" look.

"Not everything," I said. "Not everything."

He laughed. His teeth were as bad a fit as those of his look-alike at the spacepad hostel. I wondered if they were related. "No," he agreed. "Not everything."

That he should remember me was an unexpected plus. I could come directly to the point. "What's the action these days?" I said.

I'd expected recognition, what I got was an evasive "There's always action." He was looking past my shoulder and when I turned

I saw that one of the three men eating together had gotten to his feet and was coming toward us. He was direct. "Who's askin'?" he snapped at me.

I looked him over while he was not returning the favor. A tall man, nearly as tall as myself, weather-beaten face, his ears with the scarred look of ones bitten by frost more than once. On his feet mukluks of a tribal pattern I did not recognize. His eyes, unblinking on my face, trying to capture mine.

I declined the overture. I turned back to the bony cashier. "I think I'll eat before I do anything else." I said. "Got anybody to take my gear up to my room?"

He was out from behind his desk and had his hand on my para bag almost before I was through asking. "I'll take it up myself. . . ."

"Hold it," Mukluks said in my ear. He was talking to the old man. "You know him?"

The old man nodded. "He used to come in here all the time when the base was open." He had my bag and was edging toward the narrow flight of stairs to one side of his desk.

It was my turn to say "hold it" to him. I slipped my camera case off my shoulder and held it out to him. "Take this up, too." I wanted it out of sight so that nobody would start to wonder about what was in it.

I turned back to Mukluks. "Buy you a drink?" I said. "They don't serve anything aboard the shuttle."

I saw his eyes cross for the briefest of seconds. I don't suppose it was what he expected to hear from me.

I didn't wait for an answer, but moved past him to the table at which I'd seen him sitting when I came in. I picked up a chair on the way and sat down, nodding to Mukluk's two friends who looked as nonplussed as he. Both were eating left-handed, I noticed.

I looked back over my shoulder at Mukluk, who hadn't moved from in front of the cashier's desk. I made a mental note. Slow thinker. Not normally aggressive, probably doing a job when he came up to question me. All of which was in line if Harry's beast existed and Mukluk and maybe his friends had been hired to help keep the fact quiet.

I looked back to Mukluk's table companions. I smiled. "Play much poker hereabouts?" I said.

One nodded, the other shook his head. I felt encouraged. As the old man had said, there's always action, and if these two didn't agree on it being poker, then there had to be some other outlet.

I grinned at the one who'd shaken his head. A young man, no more than twenty, his face as weather-beaten as Mukluk's, but with his ears still in good shape. Maybe the thick flaps now turned up on either side of his pointed cap had something to do with that.

I grinned and I said, "So if it's not poker, what do you do to get rid of your money on payday?"

Ear-Flaps laughed, his friend who'd nodded yes to poker scowled at me. "You anxious or something?" he said. He looked to be no older than Ear-Flaps, and as weather-beaten as both his companions. But two fingers of the hand with which he was eating had no tips and his hair was long and combed down to one side. To cover a missing ear, I guessed. He was either unlucky, or did not feel a need to respect the cold.

I made another mental note. This one was to be avoided.

Mukluks had come back to sit in his chair and stare at me. I included him in my grin, went back to looking at Ear-Flaps like I was expecting an answer to my question.

He returned my grin. "So you're looking for action?"

"Sure." No-Tips was right, I was anxious. I hadn't expected I would pick up on what I wanted to know so soon, and I hoped I was hiding my feelings well enough not to blow the chance I seemed to have been handed. "Why not?"

I'd tagged Mukluks for a slow thinker, but he came alive now.

"Who asked you to sit down?" he said. His hand was up to silence Ear-Flaps, but it was plain he was talking to me.

I included the three of them in a quick glance. No-Tips put down his fork and started to grin. I noticed the crisscrossing of scars on his knuckles and pushed back my chair. Aside from my not needing the exercise, a brawl was no way to keep my profile low.

I mumbled a vague apology for my presumption and moved over to an empty table. I had a wide choice.

I glanced back as I was pulling out a chair

to sit down. Mukluks was leaning close to Ear-Flaps. I couldn't make out what he was saying, but the sheepish look on the younger man's face was clear enough.

No-Tips was turned around in his seat and staring at me. I gave him what I hoped he'd take as a friendly nod, sat down and picked up the menu card from the table.

The old man had a sense of humor after all. There was only the one word scrawled big across its center.

"Stew."

The old man didn't look to be much of a cook, and maybe he wasn't. But he did make a good stew. The food inside me, Mukluk and his bully friends gone, I figured I'd stop and talk to him before I went up to take my chances with his room.

From the look on his face and his hurry to get away when he'd seen Mukluks coming up on me, I figured something was going on that he had to know about and I meant to to find out as much as I could short of spooking him.

I held back when I saw the well-fleshed man coming down the stairs behind him. My testy fellow passenger from the shuttle. I waited until he'd handed his key to the old man and gone on out the double doors. He was wearing only a light parka, so he either wasn't going any distance or had decent transport waiting. And since there was no place that I could see worth going to in Heyday, I opted for the transport.

I was wrong on both counts. From the window to which I'd darted, I watched him stride briskly to the end of the town's one street and strike out on the long climb to the rim of the dish in which it huddled.

I turned back to the old man. "He's either got polar bear blood or you're going to have to break out the rescue squad. He can't make it out there for long the way he's dressed."

The old man laughed. It obviously was of no concern to him. "Maybe his electric socks go all the way up." he said.

"Maybe." I leaned an elbow on his cash register. To have been here before me my co-passenger had to have come directly and not stopped off at the spacepad hostel as I had. From the confident way he'd struck out he was either no stranger to *Thul*, or had the benefit of excellent briefing. I guessed it to be the latter.

But confident stride or not, what was there out there for him to walk to and what did it matter to me? I was here on the trail of a racing animal and a viable story, not to puzzle out anyone's walking habits. Maybe it was a ritual to keep his belt size within decent bounds.

I stared at the old man behind the cashier's desk for a long time. I didn't know how to begin. I didn't want to spook him again, but maybe with Mukluks and his crew gone. . . .

Finally I could think of no way to begin but to ask the question again. "What's the action these days?"

He looked up at me. This time he was eva-

sive in a different way. "You don't want to
know." he said.

"Come on," I said. "I don't remember you
being shy about touting me into losing my
money before. What's going on?"

"Look, I don't know what brought you back
to this sinkhole, but get it over with and get
out. Don't waste time fooling around."

I improvised. "I came back to take a few
pictures and maybe work up a story about the
old base. You know, a 'what's it look like now'
sort of piece."

"I didn't think the station was ever that big
an operation."

Combat and survival under extreme con-
ditions. And if the training camps back
among the ice-locked peaks had not been exactly orthodox, some of them, why burden a
civilian with the news now that they were
uprooted and gone?

"Not in size, maybe, but a lot of men passed
through who might want to show their fami-
lies what it was like," I said.

"You think anyone's sentimental about the
time they spent here?"

I expanded the project for him in my mind.
"Not *Thul* alone, a series. I thought I'd start
here because I knew the place."

From somewhere in the distance I heard a
booming sound and, in a moment, I was sure
I felt a tremor in the floor under my feet.

That was new, not the boom, that I recognized was from the mountains, but the
tremor. "What was that?" I said automati-
cally.

The old man did not pretend to misunderstand me. "You tell me," he said. "It's faint this time, but sometimes it shakes the glasses."

"What is it? I don't remember the ground shaking."

"I don't know. Maybe the whole ball of ice is getting ready to split."

"Is there anything going on back in the mountains?" I asked. I was thinking of geological activity, the old man wasn't. He gave me an uneasy, "Why don't you just take your pictures and get on out?" that to me was as good as if he'd said flat out that if it was action I was looking for, that was where it was.

It made sense to me. I hadn't mentioned racing to anyone, but if I had a strange and speedy animal I wanted to keep under wraps, what better place to breed and train it than in the back reaches of *Thul*'s remote mountains. I might even hire a bullyboy or two to discourage any nosing around.

"That's okay," I soothed him. "If you don't know anybody who wants my money, you don't know anybody who wants my money."

"It's not that, it's . . . well, things ain't the way they were when you were here."

I didn't say anything. He looked like he wanted to talk, to tell somebody. If I let the silence stretch out, it might be me.

It wasn't. "I'm giving you a room at the rear," he said. "Last one on the right. Quiet back there."

It would be quiet. I also wouldn't be able to see anything that might be going on out front

from it. The dining room was full of the old
man's stew smell among other things. I
opened the window, looking out on nothing
but the empty rise of snow and ice and the
rim of the dish that held the town.

The old man wasn't spilling over the way I
was hoping he might. Still, I couldn't just let
go.

"That big guy with the mukluks," I said.
"What do you suppose was bugging him?"

"You want breakfast?" the old man said.
"Powdered eggs is all we got."

I was right, it wasn't the time to press
him. I made a gesture that I hoped conveyed
modest disinterest, told him powdered eggs
would be okay and to call me in the morning.
I hadn't expected to get this far along in what
was really only an opening contact, and I was
feeling pretty good about the progress I
seemed to be making.

I was past the top landing and almost at the
door of the room he'd told me was mine before I realized I'd been palming the scar on
my head all the way up the shaky stairs.

I snatched my hand away, annoyed at it for
the times it picked to itch me. What could it
possibly find wrong with my having the good
luck to have targeted my area the first time
out?

CHAPTER 3

Someone was stalking me. Someone who knew how not to be seen against the seemingly open background of snow and ice. I'd taken to the back mountains and had been scouting them for the better part of a week on my skimdisk and on foot in the places where I dared not risk its roar bringing down an avalanche to overwhelm me. I'd already checked out what was left of the old outlying survival camps, five of them, on the odd chance that one or more of them might have been taken over by the breeding people I was hoping to locate.

I did not expect to find anything, and I didn't. But I would have gone through the same motions anyway to give substance to my story that I was aboard to work up a piece on my old station.

After our first encounter, the old man would have made a clam seem gabby, and the handful of people in town I tried to talk to looked patently relieved when I moved on, so that while it left me more or less hanging, the wariness I kept running into gave me a lift that I was on the right track.

I was looking for a trail, a track in the snow, some sign of movement. I saw more than I expected, but nothing that looked to me like someone working a racing animal cross-country.

But spotting so many fresh tracks deep in the back country had me wondering. I wondered even more when I saw the vehicles making them. Anything that would move and carry at least two men seemed to be out there probing the peaks and the valleys between. And the checkered orange-and-blue parkas of the civilian police were distinctive even at a distance. Could they be searching for the same thing I was?

But breeding animals, even for racing, had never been illegal. And why take the time and the men to do it with a ground search when an air sweep would have been so much the simpler? I made a mental note to check into it if Harry's animal story didn't pan out and I could stop being cautious about keeping a low profile.

From time to time I did see animal smoke, but when I moved in for a closer look, the body vapor rising was from a herd of the local equivalent of caribou or elk.

I moved in cautiously. Aside from not wanting to be caught in the act of sneaking up on Harry's racing beast, many of *Thul*'s animals were flesh-eaters and all seemed to be gifted with keen eyesight and an extraordinary sense of hearing. And I could vouch that some could be clever, tireless hunters. I had no wish for a repeat of the harrowing time I'd had escaping a bearlike monster that had taken it into its head to stalk me for its lunch when all I'd wanted of it then was a record of its looks for a survival tape our unit was putting together.

I'd left my skimdisk and was afoot and so was whoever was along my trail behind me. I had spotted not him, but his footprints in the snow. I'm six-four and have a correspondingly long stride. I guessed him to be shorter and, although he was trying to hide his prints in mine, there were times when he didn't make it and that doubling of the track in the snow was what I'd picked up.

The footing was good and, except for an overhanging shelf of snow here and there, reasonably clear. I'd taken off my skis, truncated military ones, and was carrying them across my back. I'd scrounged a mask and glasses from the old man to save my face and eyes from the pain and damage the cold and the sun could inflict and was letting my beard grow as added protection.

When I spotted the tracks behind me, I thought at first that I was getting close to the place I was hoping to find and that the man behind me was an outlying picket. I felt encouraged that I seemed at last to be getting someplace in my search and slowed my steps to let him overtake me.

I slowed, and so did he. His occasional misstep in my tracks by which I'd discovered him got no closer. I slowed even more, and the distance between us did not narrow.

I stopped to look back and he stayed put and it occurred to me to wonder what kind of a security guard it was who would not simply either pick me up or drive me off. It also occurred to me at about the same instant that maybe my tracker was not a guard at all.

Cameras had a way of making people skittish and I did not feel I needed that at the moment, so I'd not been carrying my working one with me on these excursions. Time enough to bring it to bear when I'd found what I was looking for.

But my record camera, smaller than a playing card and wafer thin, was always with me in its zippered pocket on the left sleeve of my jumpsuit. I slid my arm out of my mitten and roomy parka sleeve, reached across my chest, and took the small unit from its pocket.

The slit pockets on the chest of my parka were two-way ones and now I thrust my hand out through one and brought my camera up to my eye. I could not pick out anything along my trail behind me, but I made one exposure and then another for insurance. Later, with the computer of my main holographic unit to help enhance the image captured by this smaller one, I might discover something I could not now see with my unaided eye.

But the movement of camera to eye is an unmistakable one, and I turned back to my trudging with the uneasy feeling that, if my tracker was making an effort to remain hidden from me, it hadn't been smart to give in to the impulse to turn and let him know that not only did I know he was there, but I'd made a permanent record of the fact.

The back of my journeyman holo camera has a flip-up screen that lets me view an image before I store it permanently. It will also accept outside data and I'd fed it the shots I'd made of my back trail. Now in my darkened hotel room, I ran my scanner along the twin marks of my footprints, enlarging a section here and there for closer scrutiny.

My stalker had stayed with me, still hidden, even though my actions must by then have let him know his presence was no secret to me. He stopped when I stopped, moved when I moved. He vanished only when, with the lowering of *Thul*'s sun that glared but gave no warmth, I donned my skis and turned aside to make the long run down the jagged slopes and back to my skimdisk.

A straight edge on the screen. A straight edge that turned at a right angle. I outlined the area with a fingertip and touched the zoom control to maximum. Straight edges and clean right angles are rare in nature. The image of this one swelled in size on my screen.

I brought down the contrast. The sharp

whites and blacks of the sun on the snow smoothed to shaded grays, and I could make it out. A darker rectangle against the clean white background. Whoever'd followed me had done so in much the same way as he might stalk a game animal. Behind the cover of a blending shield. I did not see any of the townspeople being that field savvy, else they wouldn't be missing fingers and ears.

Someone rapped on my door. A firm rap. I fixed the image on my viewing screen, snapped it shut and dropped my camera into its case before I crossed the room to open my door. On the way, I flicked up the lights.

A short man, small paunch. He stepped inside without my say-so. My impatient fellow passenger from the shuttle.

"Baran," he said. "Name's Baran. Old man downstairs says you're a photographer."

"Pike," I said, returning the favor. "Eli Pike." He didn't need to ask the old man if I was a photographer, my camera case had been in plain sight for him to see all during our trip.

"Don't need you," he said. "Want to rent your camera."

That was blunt enough. He'd been taking his walks up the street and over the rim of the ridge for more than a week, passing me downstairs and in the hall to do it without a look in my direction. I hadn't cottoned to him on the shuttle. I didn't like him any better now.

"No," I said. "It's a special unit, not everybody can work with it."

"Afraid we'll break it? I'll pay you double what it's worth."

I'd caught the "we." So he was not as alone as he appeared to be. "It's the tool of my trade," I said. "Without it, I'm out of work."

"Triple."

I shook my head. "It doesn't matter what you offer. It takes more than money. It takes a CE license to even carry a camera. You have one?"

He looked at me. Not puzzled, just looked at me. Long. He knew about the Bureau of Personal Security's rigidly controlled licenses that applied to civilian transmitters and receivers as well as cameras, everybody did. I had mine by virtue of my SpaceNav service.

"I'll take the chance," he said.

"I won't," I said. "Aside from putting me out of work, trafficking in CE equipment is a felony."

"How about you lose it in an avalanche?"

It was my turn to look long. His eyes were brown, expressionless under scanty brows. I thought of the overhanging snow, the sharp ice ledges poised, in whose shadow I now prowled daily and wondered if this pudgy little man who looked to have denied himself little was asking a question or making a threat.

I had not taken my hand off the knob of my door when I'd opened it. Now I pulled it open further. "Don't worry about it," I said. "I'm insured."

My gesture with the door was not lost on my unwelcome visitor. He dismissed it with a gesture of his own, dropped down into my only chair. It creaked under his weight. "Don't get in an uproar, Pike. I need pictures.

I'd rather shoot them myself, but if you want in, we can work it out."

Want in. Work it out. I didn't need the scar on my head to warn me off this character. I said nothing, just kept holding the door open.

He was too impatient to take the silence long. He thrust himself to his feet and walked on past me and out, looking at me no more now than he did when starting on his walks.

I waited until his wide back had vanished into his own room before I decided it was time I had something to eat and went down to the lobby dining room.

"This Baran fellow upstairs," I said to the old man when he came to take my order. "What's he do?"

"He pays cash for what he wants."

I wanted information, not funny answers. "Come on," I said. "He walks in and he walks out and he never says hello to you or me or anybody else. Now you got to admit that's strange. What line of work is he in?"

"Mostly he minds his own business."

"You want me to walk over to your desk and mess up your register looking for what he put down after his name when he signed in?"

"Consultant. He put down consultant."

"What else?"

"Nothin', only consultant."

"Thanks," I said. "That's a help. Consultant. What kind? What company?"

"You ask a lot of questions for somebody who's only supposed to be taking pictures. You want a double portion stew like always?"

"Never mind the stew for a minute," I said

to the old man and took a shot. It wasn't exactly true, but it wasn't a lie either. "He wants me to do some work for him. I got a right to ask around first, don't you think?"

"I said he pays cash,"

"So he pays his bills. That's not all of it. I have to be careful who I hire out to. I have my license to protect." I hoped I sounded in earnest. "You saw his I.D., what's his home base?"

The old man looked around at the stairs before he answered me. He leaned his bony face close, too close. "Funny lookin' I.D.," he said. "No company name, no home base. Only his name and the word consultant on it. Picture is him with a beard and big glasses. Could be anybody."

"Any calls, messages? Anybody try to get in touch with him or the other way around?"

"Like you said, he never talks to anybody and nobody talks to him. You want that stew?"

The old man was his clammed-up self again, or maybe he didn't know any more about Baran than he'd already told me. "Yeah," I said. "Bring me the stew."

Sitting, waiting for him to shuffle back with my meal, I thought of the head I'd seen rise up over a hillock to look after me when I took my skimdisk cross-country the day I came aboard, and wondered if there was any connection between that watcher and the one the image of whose stalking blind I had locked in my camera.

CHAPTER 4

I was tired of the boomtown that had gone bust. I was tired of another marrow-chilling day prowling the back mountains with no results. I was tired of the old man's stew.

While I had the feeling there was more to Harry Judd's talk of a super-fast animal than just talk, I couldn't afford to be a do-or-die crusader who gets his story come the proverbial hell or high water.

I was lying on my bed, thinking how maybe I owed it to myself to write off the time and money it was costing me to chase down this racing beast story and salvage what I could from being on *Thul* with perhaps a piece on the police activity I'd been running across, when the communicator on the stand beside me went off in my ear. I picked it up.

A woman's voice, young sounding, no particular accent, and speaking so softly that had we not been on a land line I would not have been able to make out her words. "Are you the photographer?"

I was surprised. I had seen no women among the handful of stony faces turned toward me in what remained of Heyday. She had to be a new arrival.

"Yes," I said. "I'm a photographer. Eli Pike. What can I do for you?"

There was a silence on the other end of the line.

"Yes," I repeated.

It was the first time anyone was getting in touch with me. I pulled open the nightstand drawer, groped for something on which to write, found nothing. I would have to remember.

"Mr. Pike, you've been asking questions. . . ." Her voice trailed off.

I hadn't been asking question straight out, but I suppose it would not be hard to figure out what I was after if you already had the answer. If she knew that and also that I was looking for information, then maybe she wasn't as new to *Thul* as I'd supposed.

I thought I caught a note of hesitancy under the softness of her voice. I tried her with an encouraging, "Yes?"

"I . . . I think I can help you if . . . if you will help me."

I nodded sympathetically, but of course she couldn't see that. "Yes," I said. "What did you have in mind?"

She seemed to be having trouble with what she wanted to say. I didn't want her to hang up on me if she was having second thoughts. I smiled. She couldn't see that either, but I hoped the sound of it would be in my voice.

"Look," I said. "Ms. . . ?"

"Morgan, Claire Morgan."

"Ms. Morgan, suppose you tell me what it is you want me to do for you, and we can perhaps go on from there."

I heard her catch her breath before she spoke. "Could you . . . I mean, are you free? Could you see me now?" she finished in a rush.

I looked around my room. I've seen swankier places, I've been in cleaner ones. I looked out my one blank window at the evening dark gathering outside. I knew the killing cold of *Thul*'s approaching night and the last thing I wanted was to be caught out in it. "Of course," I said. "Where would you like us to meet?"

I heard the line get that pressing, closed sound it makes when you put your finger on the silencing button. So she was not alone and did not want me to hear what she was saying.

She came back on, still speaking softly, giving me directions to follow the main street along the way I recognized as the one which I'd seen Baran take to vanish over the rim of Heyday's shielding saucer.

"And bring your camera," she said before she hung up, and her words did not have the sound of an afterthought.

* * *

She was waiting, as she'd said she would be, just over and beyond the rim of the dish-shaped hollow that protected the town from the knifing wind into which I mounted step by step.

The needle-shaped skimmer in which she sat seemed in roaring high speed motion even while standing still. Over her shoulder I saw the answer to the mystery of how Baran could survive *Thul*'s debilitating temperatures wearing only a light parka. He was in the back seat, leaning forward, his grin at me triumphant.

I don't like being threatened, even obliquely, and I was remembering his talk of an avalanche and my being caught in one. I grinned back at him, glad now that I'd ignored the admonition to bring my camera which his female companion had given me.

She was holding the door open for me and I slid into the welcome warmth of the seat beside her. Her scent was clean, crisp, barely discernible. I noticed the skimmer's cabin light had not come on with her opening of the door and I wondered if she had turned it off to keep its reflected glow from being seen.

From her voice on the land line, I'd expected a petite woman. Even sitting, Claire Morgan looked tall. Tall and slender and without the large-boned angularity usually associated with women of her exceptional height. She wore a white jumpsuit and a white cap pulled down over hair the spiked ends of which, escaping, looked, in the light her dash cast upward, clearly red. I had the thought that, dressed as she was, if she stepped out of her skimmer, she would disappear against the harsh white of the snow.

"Where's your camera?" Baran demanded. Then to the young woman beside me, "I thought you told him to bring his camera."

"It's dark out there," I said. "Why would I want to carry my camera around in the dark?"

"You can shoot in the dark, can't you?"

"Of course, but only as far as my lights can reach, and that's not all that far."

"I meant infrared."

"Infrared?" I looked at Claire Morgan. Her eyes were brown. With her hair, I would have expected green or blue. "If you want me for a surveillance job, forget it. I don't hire out for that kind of work."

"You don't snoop." Baran said it sarcastically, so maybe I'd been less circumspect than I thought in my asking around.

I kept my eyes on Morgan. It was she who'd called me. I waited to hear what she had to say.

"Please, Theodore," she said to Baran. Then, to me, "You can take pictures in the dark?"

Pictures in the dark. It didn't matter which of them said it, it came to the same thing. A job more suited to the talents of an investigator than a photographer. I told them so.

"You don't understand," she said. She looked over at Baran in the rear seat, but he'd settled back in the shadows. I could not see his face. I thought he shook his head.

A gust of the night wind outside shook the skimmer. It reminded me how precipitously *Thul*'s temperature dropped once the sun was down. If I stopped ignoring the scar on my head and climbed out of my seat now, I could be over the rim of the saucer and back in the shelter of my room in scant minutes.

She was trying me out with a shaky smile. White teeth catching a highlight in the full red crescent of her lips. "I don't understand what?" I said.

"I have a sister," she said. "An older sister . . . she was always good with animals . . . she took prizes."

Her tone made it hard to tell whether she was asking me or telling me. It was her story, but I nodded. My ears stood up a little at her mention of animals though. Baran was quiet.

"She loved to race. Across country . . . steeplechase, I think you would call it here."

"I wouldn't call what Meta does steeplechase, Claire." Baran cut in from the back seat.

"So she doesn't ride the beasts . . . what else would you call it?" she flung at him.

"I wouldn't call it steeplechase."

If these two were in something together, they weren't acting like either of them enjoyed it.

Claire Morgan's gloved hands were on the wheel of her skimmer. I watched her fingers working. Steeplechase, I was thinking. A race over a course studded with obstacles. Walls, streams, even ravines. Harry's beast that could run, swim, even fly!

"Racing," I prompted. "Your sister?"

She looked over her shoulder at Baran. After a moment he shrugged his meaty shoulders and settled back again.

"My sister," she said. "She bred her own animals and ran them. With good profit, too, until her breeding pens were destroyed."

"Fire?" I said. "She was burned out?"

"No. Her stock came down with an acute disease that wiped them out in hours. From the speed with which the virus acted, she was sure it was lab-designed. At any rate, all her animals, even the ones that appeared uninfected, all had to be destroyed ... and their pens as well."

I frowned sympathetically, but I was puzzled. If she wanted to hire my camera to catch a culprit in the dark, it was a classic case of locking the barn door too late. If her sister's stock and her pens were gone, and assuming it was not a natural disease that had wiped them out, what was there for anyone to come back to destroy further?

"What is it you want of me?" I asked. This did not sound to me like Harry Judd's breeding consortium.

Baran cut in from the back seat, sounding as impatient now as he had aboard the shuttle. "Her fool sister came here to find new breeding stock and start over again. We traced her as far as Heyday and then she just evaporated."

Racing animals? On *Thul*? Harry could still be right.

"Back in the mountains." Baran was saying. "The natives. They have a hunting animal that Meta heard about and there was no holding her. Claire got worried when she stopped hearing from her sister and came to look for her. When she didn't find her, she called me."

Natives in *Thul*'s ice-locked back country? Well, maybe. I remembered we'd seen some signs when I was stationed here. Would a woman from outside vanishing from their town and being looked for make the few townspeople so nervous they would refuse to talk about betting action to someone who was no real stranger to their planet? Maybe, again, but of this I wasn't too convinced.

"I see," I said. I didn't, but I was expecting Baran would be too impatient not to get to his point. "And you need my camera to. . . ?"

"Infrared is heat. We've been looking in the daylight and finding nothing. I figure at night we can point your camera around and see what it picks up."

I looked at Claire. She'd been concerned enough about her sister to come to *Thul* looking for her, so I couldn't be sure how she would take what I was about to say. But I had to point out what to me was obvious.

"Heat?" I said. "Do you expect to pick up the body heat of a woman who has been out in the overnight cold for . . . how long?"

Baran had come aboard with me, so it had to be weeks.

He leaned forward to look pointedly at me. "Meta's not dead. She's a survivor. No, we're looking for a hot spot we can come back to in the daylight. We're not getting anywhere the way we are."

Except that no matter what Baran said, I didn't believe Meta had survived. But it was a good opening gambit. Maybe if I'd had closed transport instead of an open skimdisk, I might have ventured out at night with my camera myself. I wondered why the police I'd seen combing the area hadn't thought of it as well. But then I didn't know what it was they were looking for, did I?

I looked at Claire to see if she was buying Baran's proposition that her sister was surviving out in *Thul*'s nights.

It was possible, I knew that. I'd made the training videos that said so. But they were meant to give a man who was down and lost anyway a chance to survive. And it was at best just that, a chance. I did not see anyone, man or woman, no matter how determined, making it on a personality trait alone.

A booming sound came faintly through the walls of the closed cabin and a moment later, I felt what was by now a familiar tremor in the ground on which the skimmer rested. If Baran or Claire noticed it, they gave no sign. Her brown eyes under their arching brows stayed level on mine.

Steeplechase that was not steeplechase, breeders that were not a syndicate operation but obscure natives. A woman who could calmly accept the thought that the sister she cared for enough to follow to a frozen planet might most assuredly not be alive.

I brushed at my head with my fingers, pretending to be settling the watch cap that I wore. I do not like to let people see me rub at the scar on my scalp. "When did you want to start looking?" I said.

We'd been scouring areas of *Thul* into which I did not recall even the most far-ranging of our SpaceNav survival training field trips ever venturing, yet Baran and Claire were orienting their pointing of my camera around landmarks with which they seemed to have a more than nodding acquaintance. My suggestion that she hire a flier for more efficient coverage had been met with a silence I did not grasp until I remembered that the guards also seemed unwilling to take to the air in their search for whatever it was the civilians were after.

I was picking up hot spots in surprising numbers only to have Baran dismiss each with no more than a glance. While I was glad to be out of the cold as well as being paid to go on with a search I'd all but abandoned, I wondered why he and Claire needed me to find a particular place for them in the dark when, if they were as familiar with our surroundings as they appeared, they could not go directly to it in the daylight.

Baran, with his usual impatience, answered my unasked question, at the same time adding to my growing doubt that the search for Claire's sister would in the end lead me to Harry's racing beast.

"They moved the damn thing," he spat out, breaking the muffled silence in which we rode under a sky barren of moons.

With a skilled hand at the controls, a skimmer of this one's power could be made to leap even a sizable chasm. And time after time Claire did just that, making my throat grow tight in anticipation of her misjudging her arc and sending our needle shape smashing too low into the opposite wall. But now she was threading her cautious way across the choppy sea of broken ice fallen from the massive peaks towering on either side, an area that acquired an eerie look of flatness in the general starlight from a canopy strewn solid with diamond dust that cast no shadows.

"There it is!" Baran's sudden outcry in my ear startled me.

I looked at the flipped-up screen of my holo camera. I wasn't shooting permanent images with it, using it at its infrared setting only as a scanner. He was pointing a fat finger over my shoulder at what looked to me merely like a lighter patch off to one corner of my image. I narrowed my angle to zoom in on it.

"No, no," he said into my ear. "Here, right here."

He was leaning over the back of my seat now, crowding Claire aside with his bulk. He jabbed at my screen, his ungloved finger leaving a greasy mark.

"Back off," I snapped. I had caught some of

his excitement, but it riled me to see my camera marred even with a smudge that I knew would rub off.

I broadened my angle of view a little. I saw nothing at the spot to which he'd pointed. No brightening of the monochrome image that could be interpreted as the heat of an animal body or even radiation from equipment hidden by the mantling snow.

I pulled the frame back a little more. Nothing. In fact, the area seemed to fan out darker and colder than the ice and snow in which it was centered. "I don't see any heat coming off anything." I said.

"Are you sure that's it?" Claire was asking Baran. I felt her bring the skimmer to a stop. The tugging wind rocked the closed cabin with its gusting once it settled completely. They both seemed to have forgotten that I was there.

"I helped build it, didn't I?" Baran said, but he turned to me. "Give me a printout of that shot, and another with your maximum wide angle." And when I handed them to him, he turned on the overhead cabin light briefly to study each in turn and then nod to Claire. "Mark the coordinates and then let's get out of here."

The map case light on her dash blinked redly as she did so. "I hope you're right, Theodore," she said. "we weren't able to find it on our own, you know."

Her remark puzzled me. We left the old man's hostel at separate times, Baran and I. That I understood. But if we came back to ex-

plore this spot in the light only to find we'd
been the victims of a false reading, did she
think I would pull out of the search and leave
them to go it alone?

"I helped build it, didn't I?" Baran said to
her again and this time it seemed to satisfy
Claire. At least I saw her nod as she started
up the skimmer again.

From Claire's story of her missing sister
and their manner which to me seemed more
impatient than concerned, I'd concluded they
expected she'd found her way to the breeders and that was where she would be when
we located them ourselves.

But Baran's actions were a mystery to me.
Maybe I'd been wrong about what I had been
hired to locate with my camera. Maybe while
I was looking for the heat of breeding pens,
he'd been leaning over my shoulder keeping
an eye out for something else, for something
I did not fathom.

The spot that had Baran excited showed no
reading of warmth at all, yet there was no
doubting his certainty that he'd found what
he was looking for. I shrugged mentally. I'd
know, I told myself, when we came back for
a daylight look.

I felt the skimmer slowing and, surprised,
peered out into the dark outside for a reason.
Snow and bits of crystal ice slashed at the
cabin window, carried on a wind whipping
through what looked through the vision-
obscuring rising swirls like a narrow valley
between steeply climbing walls.

We came to a jarring stop, no smooth landing here. I turned in my seat, questioningly, to look at Claire. "This place all right?" she said over her shoulder to Baran.

He peered out one window and then the one opposite. "Fine," he said. "This will do fine."

I saw Claire nod and punch at her dash. Behind me the door began to open. The outside wind invaded the cabin in a sweeping rush to make her and Baran, who were facing it, blink. The back of my neck was suddenly chill with more than the shivering blast.

"Out," Claire said. And when I shifted my uncomprehending stare from her level brown eyes to Baran, it was to meet the small bore muzzle of the needle gun in his hand waving in my face.

"Out," Claire repeated, matter-of-factly.

The chill was cutting through to the pit of my stomach. "No," I said, groping for my mental bearings. "You can shoot me. I'm not getting out into that."

"Suit yourself," Baran said. "You can climb out while we're standing, or I can maim you a little, pick up some speed and dump you out. It's your choice."

I stared from one to the other of them aghast, searching for some sign that would tell me they were not serious. They were blinking against the wind swirling in, but that was all the expression I could read in either face.

"Is this what you did to your sister?" I finally said to Claire.

She smiled, an unpleasant parting of her red

lips. I'd never before noticed how pointed her incisors were. "I'm afraid I wasn't being truthful with you about that. You see, I don't have a sister."

"And there are no breeding pens." Baran added from behind his needle gun. His smile was as cold as Claire's when I shifted my stare to him. "Don't look so surprised." he said. "You were looking to find a racing animal. We simply tailored our story to what you wanted to hear." He motioned with his gun, "Now get out."

Slowly I started to close my camera. "Leave it," Claire snapped at me.

"Let him take it," Baran cut in. "Do you want to be caught with contraband if somebody stops us?"

"I'll risk it," she said without looking at him and waved me out with an impatient gesture of her gloved hand.

I finished securing my camera, snugging down its outer protective covering firmly, against what I did not know. Aside from being the tool of my trade, it had for me a price measured in sacrifice and sentiment and the instinct to preserve it was strong.

My hands on my camera, I looked from one to the other of them. "Tell me," I said. "What is it I'm supposed to have seen that you want to keep secret badly enough to put me out to freeze?"

For answer, Claire reached inside her white jumpsuit and when her hand came out she held a smaller version of Baran's needle gun.

Any thought I might have had to contest him for his died as it was born.

"Out," she said. "You're letting in the cold."

I'd been riding with my parka thrown open. I closed it over now, pulling its hood over my head and watch cap. The mittens were in a side pocket, I drew them on, too.

"Stop stalling," Baran said from the back seat. "You're only prolonging the agony."

"So shoot me," I said and laughed. "Kidding, I'm only kidding." I gave my camera one last pat and turned in my seat to face the door opening. The blast of freezing air was coming in with a force that made it a struggle for me to obey the prodding I felt hard at my back. Claire was getting as impatient as Baran.

I dropped the short distance to the ground, feeling myself sink deep in the snow as I landed. Barely waiting for her door to close, Claire blasted her skimmer away, its muffled roar all but lost in the sound of the wind whipping about me.

Shielding my face and eyes as best I could with an upraised arm, I watched the white-painted needle disappear almost at once amid the swirls of the snow in which I stood hip deep. Wind chill factor numbers raced through my head. Numbers racing until I thrust them brusquely aside. If I was to freeze to death in the remote wasteland of *Thul*'s back mountains, what did it matter that I'd figured out the precise degree at which that happy event had come about?

* * *

Wind chill. I had to get out of the killing wind that was draining my body of its animal heat. Claire had chosen her spot well. The steep walls on either side channeled the wind and I could see nothing to get in the lee of to shelter me from its lethal bite. Yet if I was to survive at least until light, I had to have shelter from it and quickly.

Overhead I knew the sky was crisply clear, but it could have been banked over solid with clouds for all I could see of it through the snow swirling about me. But I saw little point in looking to its stars to guide me out, their pattern shifted strangely with the seasons and there was no north star on which to fix a sighting. But the weak sun, rising, would at least show me the direction of *Thul*'s east.

I saw less point in wasting my energy floundering through the heavy drifts to find a place out of the wind until I collapsed. I would make where I stood, hip-deep in the snow, do.

With my mittened hands I began to dig. Like a terrier going to ground I dug, moving the snow up and packing it as best I could. My need was pressing, but I forced myself to work unhurriedly, careful that I did not warm myself overly. I could not afford the luxury of sweat. Sweat that was moisture to chill and to further channel from my body the heat I now must fight to conserve within it.

I had it hollowed out at last. A sheltering burrow in the snow into which I hunkered down out of the breath-snatching wind. A wind that even as I peered out into it was adding to the insulating layer atop me. I could not wait out the darkness in restoring sleep for the double reason of having to keep awake to poke clear my breathing hole as well as not falling into that last warm drowse out of which so few awoke.

Last of all, I pulled my arm free of my parka sleeve to feel at the back of my belt my sailor's dirk, that flat, straight-bladed hiltless knife that I'd learned to carry in my SpaceNav days and which more than once served to save me from being dragged down by tangled shrouds and fouled lines. It was a tooth, a small tooth against the saber fangs of the cold and of predators, but it was a tooth.

I settled myself in my small burrow, wondering if, when morning came, I would be here to emerge from it, shaking myself free of the blanketing snow, as I'd seen sled dogs do in numberless videos.

CHAPTER 5

With the dawn came hunger pangs. I have a particular problem with hunger pangs. I know most people feel them in the pit of their stomach, but in my case they're what I suppose the medics would call "referred." When I get hungry I get a pain in my chest. I get hungry enough and I can hardly breathe for the ache. It might help explain my double-ordering of food.

Since I did not intend to return to this burrow that had sheltered me through the long night, I took care of what was necessary out of the wind before I poked my breathing hole large enough for me to crawl out into the growing light. It would be hours before the sun's weak rays reached between the tall peaks, cutting it off from my direct view, but its rising glow was marker enough for me now. I put the lightening sky to my left and struck out for the calmer ground to the south. Between the sun, when it came at last into view from behind the mountain peaks, and the timepiece on my wrist, I figured I'd work out the direction that would bring me to my old base and the help of the civilian guards I'd see coursing out from it.

The wind had died down, but at each step I sank deep into the drifts. If I wasn't to wear myself out floundering through them, I had to find something out of which to make snow-shoes or skies, however crude. And nagging at me were the hot spots I'd seen on my camera screen. To me they meant openings hidden under the surface through the roofs of which my unsupported feet would break to send me plunging to my doom in their white depths.

But with the pangs in my chest making it hard for me to think straight, I knew I needed to find food before anything else.

Water was no problem. It is not a good idea to eat the snow of a strange planet for its moisture any more than it is a good idea to sample its springs no matter how unpolluted they might look. But aside from having no alternative, I'd spent time on *Thul* before and made my compromises with its beasties. I could slake my thirst with at least the hope they would not take a belated revenge.

If I could find something to burn, I should have no trouble with fire. The viewfinder of my record camera in its pocket on my sleeve had lenses I could use as burning glasses with the sun when it came up fully. But I had no hope of sending up smoke to signal my plight to a potential rescuer. *Thul*'s wind, while abating with the light, still blew strongly enough to dissipate it almost as it rose from the flame.

Tundra on *Thul* is sparse, but it is there, else all the animals on the planet would be carnivores and they are not. And where there are plant eaters, there are plants to eat. Meanwhile, it behooved me to be on the alert for animal tracks in the snow. In the severe cold, the heat-producing qualities of meat were essential.

Dawn is one of the two best times in which to hunt animals. The day ones are up to meet the sun, the night runners are returning to their burrows. At dusk, they reverse.

But hunting an animal is no easy task even for an experienced huntsman. I had no weapon except my dirk. I did, however, have the makings of a snare if I could find a trail, droppings, any sign of an animal's passing on the way to a feeding ground, across which to set it. If there were any such here, I must find them quickly and before *Thul*'s nearly constant wind rose again to sweep them away.

Alert for signs of whatever animal smoke might lead me to a feeding ground, I scoured the snow. How long and how far I could go on struggling for footing in the snow without food in my stomach or snowshoes to keep my feet from sinking into its strength-sapping softness I did not know. But with the numbing cold, I knew it could not be for long.

An animal does not develop keen sight where there is nothing to see, nor a keen ear where there is nothing to hear. *Thul*'s beasts were exceptional in both these areas of sensing. Peaks towering on all sides of me cut my vista to zero, but I could listen. Even in a wind that threatened my search for animal smoke rising, I could listen.

I did, pushing back my hood and cupping my hands behind my ears, turning my body as though they were twin dish antennae to pick up sound.

I heard it, faintly at first, then growing rapidly, a chattering sound. I had an impression of a pursuing pack. I marked its direction and turned in another. A pack chasing prey meant only one thing to me, carnivores running down meat. I did not need to meet them on their own ground.

Floundering my way to a ridge, I would slow down even more and peer over it cautiously. Eventually I got lucky. Fresh tracks in the snow, small animals from the size of the prints, many going in one direction, a few returning, an animal run I took it to be.

Threaded around the waist of my parka was a drawstring I seldom pulled snug because I liked to wear the bulky garment loose. I pulled it free of its tunnel and, working inside my parka, my hands drawn in from my sleeves, I fashioned it into a simple slip loop. When I had it ready, I climbed back to the top of the ridge. Had my string been longer, I

would have held it by an end and waited for
my breakfast to walk into my trap.

As it was, I tied the free end around a sizable chunk of ice and set my loop over the
tracks. If what caught itself in my snare was
small, the weight of the ice would be a drag
to let me catch it as it struggled to get away.
If it was larger, it would be off, taking with it
my line and my hope of capturing the food
vital to sustain me against the relentless cold
and desolation.

I slid back out of sight behind the ridge and
waited, laughing a little at the thought that
whether I ate or not, whether I survived or
not, hung in good measure on how big and
how strong was the *Thul* animal whose whim
would take it past my trap.

I waited. Because it was *Thul,* I had a small
comfort. Its animals had no keenness of smell.
I did not need to clear my trap of my scent
nor shift my position to be downwind should
it change direction.

I saw the sun now, its glare wiping out the
tip of a distant peak. It did not hurt my eyes
as yet, but I had no wish to fall victim to a
brightness that would give me no warning of
its destructive intensity until too late, until I
was snow-blind.

Stiffly, I fumbled my glasses out of an inner
pocket and put them on. I'd been lying mo-
tionless a long while, not moving lest I make
a sound to frighten away a potential victim
of my trap.

Sounds. All the interminable while I'd been
lying with no more than my eyes peeking

over the top of the ridge, I'd been hearing the sounds I took to be pack noises. Sometimes closer, sometimes distant, sometimes close enough to echo off the mountain walls around me.

But now they sounded less like predators chasing and more like animals at play. Animals played, I'd been friends with enough dogs to know that. But these were not dog sounds. These sounded to me more the chatterings of squirrels, except that squirrels did not run in packs and, so far as I knew, there were on *Thul* no animals that even resembled them.

Nor were the voices pretty. Still, lying there, hearing them, I began to listen with a sense of pleasure at the sound, now and again hearing a piping bell tone mingling. Had I been Earthside, I would have likened the feeling to the remembered pleasure of sitting on a porch, running my hounds for their needed exercise, listening to their voices echoing back to me.

Lying immobile, I'd fallen into a kind of semidaze, now I was startled out of it to realize the pack sounds seemed to be approaching just over the ridge from me.

I lifted up my head, sharply, my eyes darting first to search the distance. Then, scanning closer, I saw them. White animals, all but invisible against the snow, fewer than a dozen.

And running, running and leaping, and at a speed that made it hard for me to follow them with my eyes. Greyhound sized, but looking like no greyhound I'd ever seen, and running with a speed I'd never seen any greyhound attain.

Chasing nothing, merely running, leaping, seeming to be enjoying themselves. They did not have the look of wild animals.

One broke free, perhaps drawn by my sudden movement, and headed up the slope of the ridge in my direction. Before I could move, it was entangled in my snare and screeching its distress. It was small, whippet size. I took it to be young.

I looked toward the pack. Another animal had detached itself and was racing up the slope. In a moment it was beside the young one and nosing at it, tugging with its teeth at the drawstring that was my snare.

I lifted myself up, the older looked at me, but did not shy away. I moved closer, put out a tentative hand, fingers closed in a fist. It moved back and sat down. A beautiful female, feline looking, wrapped in a loosely hanging coat of dazzling white fur. And, from her manner, unafraid of me. She was no animal of the wild.

Watching her, I put a hand on her pup, ready to snatch it away if I was guessing wrongly. The young one stopped its struggles at the instant of my touch. It, too, seemed unafraid of me; was used to being handled.

I lifted it up from the snow, a heavy-feeling animal, eyes unexpectedly blue.

A thrust at my back. I turned. The sharp end of a ski pole. Two figures, short, barely to my chest, bulky in white fur, eyes hidden behind the slits of horn snow visors. The faces, clean under flat fur caps as white as their cloaks, not friendly.

In the hands of one, a crossbow cocked. An efficient-looking weapon, compact, fléchette tip a bright flash in the sun, pointing at my middle.

A command. A hoarse, guttural sound barked at me in a tongue I did not understand, but whose meaning I grasped well enough. I set the pup, still tangled in my drawstring snare, down gently. The ski pole gestured me away. I moved back, wary at the way the crossbow stayed tracking me.

The one with the poking ski pole thrust both of his upright in the snow. He picked up the pup, worked it free of its entanglement in my snare, slipping one hand free of its mitten to do so. I noticed he had but two fingers to oppose his thumb.

He set the freed pup down, not too roughly. Its mother gave it a chastising cuff with a dainty paw which it evaded easily and the two snow animals raced down the slope, back to the pack.

Two-Fingers barked another command at me. As before, I did not understand his words, but his gesture was plain enough. That and the fact that I saw Crossbow's cocked weapon rising.

I held out my hands, sighed inside when I saw the negative shaking of Two-Fingers' head, put them behind my back and in short order felt myself bound securely with my own snare cord.

* * *

We moved, they easily on their short skis, the snow animals romping ahead and around us. These were not dogs, nor hunting cats, but the pack analogy was unmistakable.

I'd had trouble making progress in the snow before. With my hands bound behind my back the best I could do was to try rolling to the side when I fell on my face in the hope that I could keep the snow out of my eyes, nose, and mouth.

My snow glasses were gone with my first fall. That the younger animals of their pack would run to nip and tug at me when I was down seemed to please my captors. At least their laughter, a high-pitched cackling sound that contrasted strangely with the hoarseness of their speech, made it seem so.

Two-Fingers and Crossbow fell silent once. The by now familiar booming sound came echoing off the walls of a canyon of ice through which we were moving. Almost at once I felt the ground under me move. Not with the tremble I'd grown to expect, but in a lurch. My two fur-clad captors looked at each other, the anger sparking in their eyes unmistakable.

In the near distance twin peaks loomed higher against the sky than their neighbors, here and there a darkening streak along their glistening sides. My eyes were beginning to ache with the glare and the snow I could only blink out of them. The air was growing thin, harder for me to breathe. We were climbing.

I was down again, spitting snow, struggling

to make it to my knees and to my feet when I heard from the pack that clear, bell-like cry. As if it were a signal, the romping animals abandoned their sport with me to plunge at their startling speed after their leader out of sight under what I took to be a low, shelflike overhang of snow.

A ski pole prodded me and pointed. I nodded, and when I'd made it to my feet I followed the snow animals.

Once under the overhang, I saw I'd been mistaken in thinking it merely a shelf. At the rear was a low opening with the glimmer of light beyond. I thought of the medieval practice of fashioning a portal so that anyone entering would have to bend nearly double and so present himself at a disadvantage to a defender inside it.

The opening was made small to hinder the entry of men whose heads came barely to my chest. To me, six-four and bound, it was a grunting effort to go through it.

I made it, with the help of Two-Fingers and his prodding ski pole. I made it, emerging to face the point of a spear in the grip of a guard who, except for his scanty red beard and the fact that he wore no sun visor, could have been the twin of either Two-Fingers or Crossbow. I could see his eyes and they were not friendly.

But even as I struggled with the confining aperture, I was gazing with amazement at the vista beyond it. And vista it was. I was looking down a great, level-floored valley which only began between the twin mountains. The

weak sun was just beginning to reach down
to touch the tops of a surprisingly sizable settlement of skin huts. Overhead, rope bridges
spanned the open space from steep wall to
steep wall, from ledge to ledge, cavern mouth
to cavern mouth. From the caverns I saw
heads popping out to join those now peering
from the huts.

The blast of a horn hung atop a low post
beside the portal sounded in my ear. If the
portal guard meant to alert his people to our
coming, he could have saved his breath. A
stream of fur-cloaked figures was already
racing toward us. Men in the main, a few children leaping, the women hanging back about
the huts, a considerable cluster and still
growing.

I felt myself a giant standing between Two-
Fingers and Crossbow. I pulled myself up to
stand even taller as the first of my captors'
people swept around us, their voices hoarsely
questioning.

Crossbow held up a hand, spoke rapidly to
a sudden silence. A shocked silence I sensed
it to be. I wondered what he was saying to
make the faces turned to mine all at once so
stony.

Two-Fingers was again at work on my back
with his ski pole. Prodded, I moved. The
crowding stream parted, pulling back from
us, from me. I had the feeling that I was in
some way anathema to them. That there was
something more in their silent regard of me
than simple aversion toward an unwelcome
stranger.

THE ICE BEAST 69

Two more things I noticed at almost the same glance. The clustered women were even shorter than their men and as fur-clad. But at the rim of their growing group one towered as tall above them as I did above my captors. At the same instant my eye caught movement against the near wall of the valley. A figure, two figures, a man and a mount. The man just a man, but the mount a burly looking animal, small head outstretched, and moving with a speed that to me was as incredible as that of the snow pack when I'd first seen it. If Claire's sister was indeed out to restock her racing stables, strange though this beast looked, she had come to the right place for her breeding stock.

And then I remembered. Claire Morgan's sister was only a creature of her expediency to gull me into finding for them whatever it was she and Baran were looking for and, with their dumping of me to freeze in the snow, seemed to have found.

Two-Fingers prodded me to an open square in the midst of the skin huts. He motioned me to sit and I did, crossing my legs, holding my head and back erect. Even with my hands behind my back and my wrists long numb with the tightness of Two-Fingers' tying, I did not intend to allow myself to look beaten.

On the faces circling me and Two-Fingers and Crossbow, who'd each dropped to a semi-squat on either side of me, I saw an abhorrence I had not encountered even during the darkest of my SpaceNav duty days.

I sat, tired from my efforts and the exposure and with the unaccustomed stiffness of my position, and I waited. I waited along with the villagers, grown now to be numbered in the scores if I'd been counting, and all of them still oddly silent.

A murmur rising, their hearing as sharp as that of their animals, they'd heard it before I did. A rhythmic pounding and, seeming to come out of the snow and the ice of the wall itself, two men, the messenger and one other appeared, each mounted on a burly riding beast.

Their speed had them upon us in a moment, the crowd parting to let them through. An armed man this new one also, the long hilt of the two-handed sword angled across his back high above his shoulder. A chief I took him to be from the deference with which Cross-bow rose to take hold of his bridle. He did not dismount, but looked down on me from his high saddle.

Up close, the mounts appeared to be as loosely pelted as had the snow animals of the pack. Small, feline heads also, but unpretty. The one held bared his teeth in a twisting motion to seize the hand on his bridle and I saw the long incisors flash. The movement did not appear to be unexpected, Crossbow letting the powerful neck lift him from the ground, but not loosening his grip on the braided leather strap.

Two-Fingers was on his feet, his hoarse voice rising, pointing at me, gesturing with his hands, The chief listening, sitting tall in his saddle, not nodding, his eyes steady on me all the while.

From the motions of Two-Fingers' hands and body, his gestures in my direction, I gathered that whatever heinous act it was that had shocked his cohorts to sudden silence had to do with me and the snow pup I'd snared in the cord that now bound my wrists so tightly.

Sacred animals were nothing unique in the galaxy. An Earthside dog, I recalled, once of the size and valor of a lion, had with the coming of gunpowder lost its function on the battlefield but kept its hold on the hearts of its warlord masters. They bred it down until it was small enough in size to be carried in the sleeves of their mandarin robes and made its possession by any of a lesser caste punishable by death. Had I, without knowing, violated just such a taboo?

The chief turned in his saddle, asked of the circled crowd what sounded to me a single question, his voice as guttural as that of Two-Fingers. His answer was a shout, from the men only I noticed, and a nodding of fur-capped heads.

The woman who was taller than the others had not taken her eyes from me since I'd come, Two-Fingers prodding me, down the trail into the valley. Her hair under her cap looked as red as Claire Morgan's and she was easily as tall. Now, at the rising shout, her full lips parted. I saw the thin nostrils flare, a look of pleasurable expectation flooding her dark to blackness eyes.

Two-Fingers and Crossbow had me under the arms and were lifting me to my feet. They thrust me forward to follow the chief, who'd wheeled his animal about and looked to be heading back toward the wall out of which I'd seen him and the returning messenger appear to materialize.

I staggered with my first few steps, stiff with the fighting of the snow and the cold and with my long sitting.

The fur-clad cohort moved with us, growing to a pushing, shoving crush as others joined the cavalcade from the mouths of high caves and of hidden valleys we passed. The guttural voices not silent now, and in them a note disquieting to my inner ear. A carnival note as of a circus spectacle anticipated.

The exultant anticipation I'd seen flood darkly into the tall woman's eyes at the chief-answering shout of my captors rose sharply in my mind.

Exultant, leaping anticipation . . . and in my ears the carnival sounds swelling.

CHAPTER 6

The crowd sensed blood, my blood, and roared its approval at the prospect. The echo of a thousand shouting throats and more resounded from the ice walls rising to cathedral-like arches high overhead. From somewhere among them I heard a woman scream, a feral sound that made the hair rise up on my neck.

Their circled mass surged close to the dais on which I, freed of my bonds and the doom of the icy vat by the man I called the Jester, stood facing their champion.

Their tribal champion, stripped to a kiltlike rag about his hips, barrel-stomached and thick through his chest, outweighed my two hundred pounds by at least another thirty. I had the longer reach, but that was all I had. There was no way I was going to take him in any kind of primitive grappling and, from the spread of his grin, he knew it. And the faces of the mob pressing close told me they knew it, too.

I looked out over them, the heavy stink of their blood lust flaring my nostrils, turning me away from the sight of it in the skull look of their grins, in the bright glitter of their eyes.

I looked at the Jester sitting cross-legged at one corner of the dais floor and he was grinning, too. Even Two-Swords, his chief, seated atop his drum, the loser in the test of wills I felt I'd witnessed, even he was grinning.

I came back to their tribal champion grinning at me all the way to his yellow back teeth. He stamped both his feet, planting them firmly, and held out his thick arms to me, inviting me closer. It was plain he meant to please himself and the crowd at my expense before he got down to proving, on my body, how guilty I was of my accused offense, how unworthy of mercy.

Somewhere the woman with the feral voice screamed again. I searched for her, and when I found a face I took to be hers among those pressing to the front, I did not feel surprise that I should recognize it as that of the tall woman in whose dark eyes I'd seen anticipation surge.

Single out one person in your audience, and play to him . . . to her. And I would.

I am six-four. Flabby and balding, but still six-four. I pulled myself up to stand as tall as

I could and spread my arms wide to the crowd for silence.

I waited, my mind and heart racing and, after a long moment they gave it to me, mingled here and there with a nervous catching of breath, a choked-off laugh. It was a given with them, I was certain, that in no way was I going to best their man. The end was inevitable no matter how I squirmed to hold it at bay, but to watch my frantic, futile flounderings to do so, could only add a fillip to their merriment. They sensed spectacle and seemed willing to let me play out my poor preliminaries to it.

The cords that had bound me spread-eagled in the vat still lay at my feet, I bent down and scooped up the severed lengths. I kept three and flung the rest aside.

Moving slowly and with deliberation, I coiled a length smoothly on itself and gripped the formed loop between my teeth. A murmur ran through the crowd. I took it to be one of curiosity and amusement.

I did the same with a second length. The third and shortest I looped over my left wrist, laid my right one across it and looked over at the Jester, considering. I did not know why he acted to save me from certain hypothermal death in the icy vat in apparent defiance of his chief, but if he was the juggler I suspected him to be, he could well recognize what I was about and I would be lost. But then, if I'd read his contesting of the will of Two-Swords aright, he might know and still choose not to betray me.

Excitement rising in me, I took the critical chance. I walked to the corner where he sat cross-legged and held out my hands for him to bind the cord tight.

He did not move. For moments while I counted my heartbeats he did not move. I knelt and held out my hands and the binding cord to him again.

His eyes locked on mine. Blue. Blue as the ice of which the walls and vaulted ceiling of this cathedral cavern were formed, and cold as the thin air chilling on my skin.

And then he leaned forward, took hold of the cord ends and pulled them tight. Tight until my bonds gouged deep into the flesh of my wrists and tied them off with a knot that wound back and in on itself until I knew it was one he meant not to be untied.

When he was finally through, I got to my feet and crossed the dais to Two-Swords and held out my bonds for his inspection.

Like the Jester, Two-Swords took his time. He waited for me to kneel and hold out my hands to him a second time as had the Jester. After a long moment during which I saw his eyes were not on me but studying the man across the dais from him, he took hold of the knot between his fingers. He tugged at it, tried to get a fingernail under the cord cutting into my wrist, could not, finally nodded and dismissed me with a wave of his hand.

I stood up. I stood up and made the round of the dais. All four sides of it. At each side I held up my arms and showed my hands tightly bound. I could feel the pounding of my pulse, but I moved slowly, setting an almost dragging pace.

The crowd was silent, surly almost. Was I exhibiting high contempt for their champion in that I meant to take him with both my hands tied? Or had I resigned myself to the inevitable and was I now stalling for time?

Did I, in letting myself be bound, mean not to fight him back; mean to deprive them of the full measure of enjoyment in their anticipated spectacle?

I sensed their impatience rising and risked it spreading as long as I dared. I was building a mood, a leisurely tempo, an expectation in those whose eyes and minds I must hold captive. I would have but the one chance and when it came, if it came, it would last for no more than half a gasp's time and I must act to seize it swiftly. I was putting on a performance for my life.

The chamber air was icy, but when I turned at last to their champion, the sweat was forming on my face and I prayed that the flush I could feel rising in my cheeks would not betray my inner tautness to him.

I walked toward my adversary, who was standing, arms loosely at his sides, at ring center. I walked toward him, my looped cords between my teeth, fighting to keep my movements leisurely, my hands outstretched in his direction.

He took the gesture as I meant him to take it, as I prayed he would take it, that I was holding out my hands for his inspection also.

Smirking at the crowd, he started to raise up a hand to wave me aside.

I seized it. With the darting speed of a feeding lizard's tongue, my right hand whipped itself loose of its stage magician's ties and seized his rising one. My fingers curled around his extending arm at the wrist, jerking him forward, stretching his arm out as far as it would go, My other hand, my left, swept upward to strike at his elbow joint. His bellow of surprise and pain changed abruptly to a choking gasp and I felt the resistance suddenly go out of the arm in my grasp.

I kept moving on to his left, pivoting on my right foot, my left hand sliding along his arm, ramming upward into his armpit. Behind him now, I flattened it against his now ruined shoulder and pushed.

We went down together, he to his knees and slammed flat in almost the same motion, I with my knee sharp in his spine, yanking his now flaccid right arm back and up toward his neck. With my left hand I snatched a cord from between my teeth, snubbed one end around his captive wrist. Looping from the left to the right, I threw it over his head and around his throat and crossed it on itself.

He had no wind to roar full-throatedly, but his left hand was flailing the air behind him, fingers clawed to grasp me in whatever way he could. A haphazard looking movement. Perhaps with his mind-set that my hands were bound, his brain could not accept that I could possibly be doing to him what I patently was.

I captured his flailing wrist with my right

hand, yanked, and with my left, snubbed the other end of my cord around it.

He was choking now, gagging, garroting himself with his struggles pulling tight the crossed-over cord around his throat.

Raising up my right leg to swing it over his head, I pivoted on my pointed knee gouging into his back. I felt and heard a crackling, but I did not know if came from my knee or his spine.

In spinning, I lifted myself up, and when I came fully astride him, I slammed my full weight down on his back. I heard whatever breath he'd managed to draw go out of him forcibly with my heavy impact.

His feet flew up in reflex action, but it would not have mattered to me if they hadn't. Even as my body came down on his rib cage to knock what little air he had left from his lungs, I was reaching out with my long arms for his legs and feet. I seized his rising ankles, snatched the second cord from between my teeth and snaked it around them in poor imitation of a cattle tie. Poor, but it served.

I rose to my feet, and by the time I was erect and standing fully astride their fallen and bound champion, my hands were back in their magician's bonds and when I raised them high above my head, all could see the cords still gouging deeply into my flesh.

All could see and meet my gesture with sudden, stunned silence. Seconds, brief seconds had elapsed—the photographer's timer in my head had ticked off no more than twelve—absolute, stunned silence.

I did not wait for it to break. I did not know how it would break. When I circled the dais displaying my bonds before, my purpose had been a lulling one. Now I spun on one foot and went swiftly to Two-Swords sitting atop his drum.

I did not kneel this time, but thrust out my hands to him at once. His eyes, staring at my bonds, raised up to mine. He looked as dazed and uncomprehending of what had happened as any in the crowd around us.

I looked down levelly at Two-Swords from my towering height. I did not know what their custom was, but their champion did lie fallen and bound behind me. It had to mean something. I thrust my hands at him again. Demanding.

Slowly, he stretched out a hand to take the Jester's knot between his fingers. He did not examine it, he had done so before and knew he could not solve its twinings.

I watched him reach, not for the expected sword, but behind his back with his free hand and when it returned to my sight he held in it a short, flat-bladed medieval-looking dagger. A devious culture, I thought, to carry hidden a weapon that looked to be capable of piercing armor.

He sliced at the knot and it fell away. With it went a portion of the skin on my knuckles, but I did not flinch at the sudden well of blood.

I did not linger to savor my freedom. I had to get to their fallen and trussed champion before a salient fact could dawn on him. That the cords which bound him were not secured with knots. I had not taken the time to more than snub them tight with sailor's bights. They would hold him only as long as he continued to struggle and hold the cords taut.

I leaned over him, tugged at the ends, and he was free to roll over and untangle himself from the rest. Awkwardly, moaning his pain, clutching at his throat, his elbow, gripping his shoulder. I might have hurt him less were I more adept. But I am not so proficient that I can fully control what I do. It would be a while before he had the use of that arm.

Slowly, I turned in place. My hands high, arms spread wide. All could see me now free, all could see their champion, bound by me with tied hands and freed by me with a tug, moaning at my feet.

Silence. Sudden, stunned silence had gripped the crowd and held them frozen still. I heard not so much as a whisper break it. I circled them all with my eyes, ending at last with the woman whose dark eyes and feral scream had sparked my attention.

My eyes locked on hers across the chill distance, I let my body settle slowly. Slowly until I was sitting cross-legged on the dais. Head up, a wrist loose on either knee.

I was feeling the cold, feeling it to my bones. I could have reached out for the cloak their champion had put aside with which to cover my nakedness but I did not. I allowed my eyes to slowly close and in my mind went back to bask in the bubble of warmth that had served my body so well when it was spread-eagled and bound. What happened now was out of my hands . . . as it perhaps had always been.

I felt a cloak being draped over my shoulders. "Nicely done," a voice said low in my ear in clear Galactic English. I caught my start of surprise in time not to move. It was the Jester. "But now what do we do with a sorcerer?"

CHAPTER 7

I was out of the cold at last. The hut, as low as the others but longer, while not overly warm, did have a fire at its center. I had a haunch of meat in my hand that would have been too hot for me to bite into if I'd been less ravenous.

I did not have my parka back, but I did have my jumpsuit and with it my camera in its sleeve pocket. And, after a long hesitation, the Jester handed me my dirk.

"Thank you," I said and looked at him when he met my words with a blank stare.

For a moment I was perplexed. I was sure it had been he who'd leaned close on the dais and in Galactic called me sorcerer.

Then I looked about at the men crowding the long, low hut, chiefs all they looked, and

83

wondered if speaking Galactic English was an ability he did not wish his mates to know he had.

But I let it go and when he held out a flat fur cap and a vestlike garment of some white-furred animal skin for me to put on, I merely nodded my thanks and went back to my haunch of meat. I would have moved closer to the fire to ease the chill still clinging to my bones, except that the skin someone had spread for me to sit on seemed at the moment a haven the men milling about the hut seemed reluctant to approach.

There was much loud talking, much waving about of arms and pointing in my direction, but the Jester seemed the only one willing to come close to me. That suited me. I was too hungry and too worn down to fence with anyone, least of all with a group whose language I did not understand, and whose mind-set I did not grasp.

The ground lurching under me, and a moment later the boom, took my attention from my eating. Silence fell in the room.

I looked up, surprised that the lurch had come first and not the boom. Now I was hearing a crackling sound, as of the frozen earth slipping and settling. I noticed that all faces seemed to turn to the Jester before they resumed their babble.

Someone came running into the hut. The tall woman I'd first seen outside the valley huts and whose scream I'd heard in the mob at my testing. Her eyes were wide and dark and excited looking. She ran to the Jester and spoke to him in a low voice. There was no mistaking her agitation.

He listened, then turned to me, leaning close, as close as he'd been in the dais ring. "How do you feel about being a god?" he said.

I looked not at him, but at the woman. Tall, the hair escaping from under the straight-across line of her fur cap as darkly red as her full lips. "Are you Meta Morgan?" I threw at her and was rewarded by seeing those oddly dark eyes widen momentarily before she turned them blankly to the Jester.

But the split-moment widening had betrayed her to me. She'd understood me well enough. She knew Galactic and she was Claire Morgan's sister Meta. And since she was, about what else had Claire lied to me—and for what reason if she expected I would by dawn be dead?

The Jester's lips smiled at her, but not his eyes. "You saw for yourself, Meta, he is a magician."

She spoke to him, rapidly, in the tongue I did not understand. He shrugged, turned to me, repeated his question, his voice so low I had to strain to make out his words.

"A god?" I said, "What are you talking about?"

"It will take being a god for you to get out of here alive."

The woman called Meta laughed. She laughed as though the prospect of my demise were something wonderful. I thought of her animal scream when it looked as though I was about to be mashed by their tribal champion.

''That will be enough,'' the Jester said. ''Remember, it could be your neck, too.''

He turned back to me. ''These are not a superstitious people, but they believe what they see and you had to be a magician to do what they saw you do to their man. Until they figure you out, you're just hanging. Besides, you're too much of a danger for them to let you walk away.''

''Me? A danger? How?''

''To begin with, you know they exist.''

I thought of the entrance to the valley under a ledge that I would have passed without a second glance, and of a tracker who hid behind a snow-white screen. The Jester could well have a valid point.

But I'd caught what he'd said to the woman about it being her neck as well so that his concern for me did not impress me overly with its sincerity. ''Thanks a lot,'' I said, ''but I'll stay a mortal and take my chances.''

He looked at me, but said nothing. I had the feeling he would get to me later when his secret that he knew Galactic was in less danger of being exposed.

Another sound took my attention away from the Jester and Meta Morgan. Voices, many, high-pitched and swelling rapidly. Feet pounding on the path outside. Someone running, someone running for his life from the sound of it. A wild outburst of shouting that sent Meta racing toward the door and out.

The men in the room suddenly fell silent. A different silence than the one brought on by the lurch and boom. I sensed an odd feeling of discomfiture in it.

The voices were closer now and I could make them out more clearly. Make out the glass-edge note of hysteria in the sound.

A crescendo, a peaking of the cacaphony froze me in mid-motion and held me, the haunch halfway to my open mouth. A sudden violent outburst rising to end in abrupt silence. Mingled with the intense emotional excitement of the savage sound, I'd heard a hoarse crying out, a penetrating scream that pierced through more than the thin skin walls of the hut.

"What is it?" I demanded of the Jester. The sound was hackle raising, vivid, startling, sharp. A note of hysteria.

He was silent, his fingers working the wand with which he'd poked my ribs in the vat. All in the hut were silent. I saw the gathered chiefs looking about, but not meeting each other's eyes. In a while, their voices came back, but not with the same vehemence. They seemed subdued, embarrassed. In a while they began to file out singly, in pairs, and in small groups.

When the last of the gathering was gone and we were alone I turned to the Jester for an explanation. He shrugged. "You didn't expect they would give the loser a prize, did you?"

"The loser! You mean. . . ?"

"What do you think they would have done with you if you'd been the one to lose the contest?"

"A trial by arms?" I said, not fully believing. It was too backward a way to judge anyone's guilt. "What was the water tub about, then?"

"Trial by immersion. You've heard of it, I'm sure."

"I've seen the history tapes, yes, but. . . ."

"If you survive, you are obviously a sorcerer and must be put to death. If you don't live, you were just as obviously innocent and will be buried with all honors and regret. Your stunt with their champion has them confused and until they sort it out you're not going anywhere . . . without help, that is."

"And you're the help I must have, is that it?"

He shrugged. "You wouldn't have lived when the ice water hit you and you know it. I gave you a chance."

"Yes, so why do I have the feeling that my welfare was the last thing you had in mind when you set me up against your bullyboy?"

He spread his hands. His left palm was badly scarred. "Why else would I try to save you?"

My head was too weary for me to think of what it was he thought I could do for him now. Aloud I said. "Let me guess. You're in some kind of power tussle with the head man and you figured it wouldn't hurt you any to be a crowd pleaser and give them a bloody circus. Especially if the chief wanted to go the traditional route and just let me die."

I'd had my fill of the meat. It was just as well, there was very little left on the bone. I looked about for something on which to wipe my fingers.

"Use your vest front," the Jester said. "Thanks," I answered and rubbed them against the ground.

He fell silent, he may have been thinking. At the moment, I didn't care. I'd been through a lot, I was ready to sleep. I fell over on my side, right where I was was good enough. I'd slept in rougher places.

But he wasn't about to let me rest. He had me by the shoulder, shaking me and calling me by name.

He was calling me by name. I took offhand note of the fact without really wondering about it. He'd had my jumpsuit with my record camera and CE license. He could have read it off that. Or maybe recognized me from when I'd been stationed here. It would not be the first time somebody I could swear I'd never seen before had come up to me and called me by my name.

But no matter, if he wanted something from me, I wanted something myself. I wanted sleep and I would have it.

I tucked my arms against my chest and blotted the Jester's poking from my consciousness. It was the least of what I needed to blot out. There was the echo of that scream outside the hut for me to work on.

That and the thought that it could still be mine.

CHAPTER 8

Two-Swords was Uldhaar, and he was chief of chiefs. The Jester was Sten and, although I still had to hear it from her, Meta was Meta. And I'd caught up on the sleep I'd lost fighting off the killing cold of *Thul*'s long night enough to sit up without my eyes closing.

My crime had been a double one. Not only had I trapped a chief's hunting animal, but I'd done so with a snare. The first was a forgivable offense, but the setting of a trap or a snare was not. Sten's people figured there were more than enough natural hazards without adding man-made ones to injure a prized animal or snag a hunter's ski or otherwise maim him enough to make him easy victim to a marauding carnivore or the ever-present cold. It was a rigid taboo and I was in no way sure I was clear of it.

They let me move about more or less as I wished, and that alone worried me even with the two guards they set to be with me all of the time. Crossbow men both, who could bring me down at a distance. After my performance on the dais, it looked like no one, except Sten, was willing to risk coming within arm's reach of me.

I was busy with my record camera, but I thought twice before I shot once. There was much I would have liked to photograph, but while I made it a practice to keep my power packs fully charged, I did not know when next I would have access to an energy source to recharge this one. And, considering how jealous they seemed to be of keeping their existence hidden, the fact that no one tried to stop me from shooting did not sit easy with me. They either didn't know what I was doing, or, more unsettling to me, they didn't care. I could burn tape on anything I liked, who was going to see it, was the thought that kept pushing itself into my mind.

Sten had not brought up the god business after his one remark, but maybe, with the guards there, he was just waiting for a better chance.

But if he wasn't ready to talk to me, I was more than ready to talk to him. I had not forgotten the racing animal story that had brought me back to *Thul*, and the first chance I got I wandered over to the pens where they stabled the ugly-tempered animals they rode.

I could not talk to their keepers about them,
of course, but I kept close watch of the way
they handled their charges and it wasn't long
before I began to wonder if part of their
beasts' ill temper wasn't due to their natural
dislike of the high saddles the chiefs used.
They snapped and bit when saddled up, but
seemed docile enough when the stable boys
rode them bareback.

Sten misunderstood my interest or maybe
he didn't. "Forget it," he said. "You couldn't
get close enough to steal one if you tried, and
if you made it, it would probably eat you the
first time you tried to climb onto its back.
They're carnivores, or hadn't you noticed."

"I noticed," I said, and looked around for the
guards. They were by the open door, their
eyes on me, but there was a lot of snorting
and other animal noises going on so I took
the chance.

"Listen," I said to Sten, not looking at him
and talking low. "You said something about
getting me out of here. What did you have in
mind?"

He didn't answer for a long moment and I
thought that maybe he hadn't heard me. But
then he reached up a hand to take hold of a
bridle and when the animal did not bare its
teeth I was sure it was the saddles.

"I'm thinking about it," he said. "I'll let you
know."

I almost forgot myself and stared at him. I
hadn't expected so casual an answer. I had
also not forgotten that the chiefs had not
made up their minds about me. "Hey," I said.

"How much time do you think I have to sit around and wait?"

He let go of the bridle and his eyes, when they moved across my face, were as blank as Meta's when she was not letting on she knew Galactic.

I followed him out the door and toward the hut and the pad that seemed to be my home base, trailed by my two keepers. There was a fire going there, tended by one or two of the older women, and a roast waiting for me to eat. I would have liked to think they were putting themselves out for me, but I had the feeling that the hut, aside from being the village long house, was also a stopover place for whatever chief happened to be passing through and wanted to get in out of the cold.

We walked without talking. Suddenly, for no good reason that I could think of, I found myself not wanting to breathe the air. It was not the cold thinness or its lack of oxygen that was bothering me—I had by now grown used to that—but a hanging stillness that was an electrical charge and yet was not.

I stopped noticing the air when I felt the ground under me lurch heavily and saw the huts sway for the first time with the force of the movement. But the booming sound did not follow. I heard only a grind and a crunch that seemed a distant sound yet came oddly from under my feet.

Sten had been knocked off his feet, as was one of the guards. It was by far the heaviest shock I remembered feeling. Sten's face was grim. He barked something at the guards in

the hoarse language I did not understand.
Both men hesitated, looked at me, then ran.
Heading, I saw, in the direction of the pens
where the riding beasts were stabled.

Sten was sending out messengers. To whom
and why I could not guess, but from his face,
it looked a serious enough reason for him to
countermand the order to keep me under
guard and for the crossbowmen to obey.

When they were out of sight he turned to
me. I'd stared across enough poker tables to
know the look of a man who didn't like what
he saw in his hand but was determined to play
it anyway. He took a long time studying me
before he spoke. "I hope," he finally said,
"for both our sakes that you know a few more
tricks than the rope tie you used to wipe out
poor Hagor."

People were streaming from the huts and
toward the center square of the settlement,
some running. Maybe it was the earthquake
that had shaken them up, or maybe Sten's
messengers. Sten himself was looking up and
down the path and I wondered why he
worked so hard at keeping secret from his
clansmen his knowledge of Galactic.

He read my mind. "We're not so backward
that we don't know what happens when people let outsiders mix in with their way of life.
And language is an insidious wedge, I think
you'll admit."

I saw his point, maybe better than he sur-
mised. I'd been speaking Galactic English for

so long I no longer thought in any other language.

"So if your people knew you spoke Galactic they'd figure you to be contaminated and there goes your influence," I said.

"Something like that."

Sten's voice was calm enough when he spoke to me, but his eyes were angry. I had the feeling he was being forced to improvise and he didn't like it.

"Help me with this," he said abruptly. "Believe me when I say you have no other chance of making it out alive."

I'd been more or less thinking along the same lines myself. I didn't know their customs, but I had only to remember what they'd done to Hagor to know that whatever they were, they took them seriously.

What the earth shaking had to do with what Sten wanted from me I couldn't figure. But he'd called me sorcerer and magician and mentioned tricks. I might be misreading him badly, but I didn't see him expecting me to work a supposed spell to appease an angry earth god. Or pretending to. I told him as much. I added that he'd already said his people were not superstitious.

He laughed, but the anger did not lift in his eyes. "You don't have to do a thing but sit still and look mysterious."

My ears were getting as sharp as those of my captors, or maybe it was the cold air and my being keyed up. I heard the thudding gallop and saw a pair of chiefs sweep up to the long house. The speed of their animals was phenomenal.

"What are you mixing me up in?" I said. "A power play? I won't work blind."

Sten was visibly tense. His voice dropped to no more than a hoarse wheeze. "You don't have any choice," he said. "You're not stupid, you've probably already figured out Uldhaar's not going to let you leave. The only chance you have is to follow my lead and hope it works. To get Uldhaar to step down."

"In favor of you."

"Yes, in favor of me." He took hold of my arm, pushing me toward the long house. "I don't have the time left to groom a crown prince. I don't have any time left, period."

I pulled my arm free. I don't like being pushed, physically or otherwise. "I won't work blind," I said again and I meant it. "What's pressing you all of a sudden?"

We were getting close to the long house, close enough to be heard. Impatience blended with the anger of Sten's voice. The anger was not directed at me, the impatience was.

"Look, I didn't plan to do it this way, but you felt how badly the ground moved. If Uldhaar doesn't step down, the whole planet is going to go."

"The shaking ground. Uldhaar's doing that?" If these primitives could control an earthquake, they were a lot more sophisticated technically than they looked.

"No. But he's keeping me from stopping it before it's too late."

Sten was looking at me and I could almost

see the wheels turning in his head as he tried to figure out how much he needed to trust me with. Something had forced his hand and I was having a hard time believing it was the earthquake, that he was not using it as an excuse of opportunity to wrest control of the clans from Uldhaar. I'd sensed the tension between the two. But his anger did seem genuine.

"All right," Sten finally said, and I knew he wasn't giving me the whole of it. "They saw what you did to their strongest man. I'm going to tell them the earth moving has displeased you and that if they don't side with me to do something about it, you'll feel forced to take drastic action of your own."

He hesitated, then said, "I'm staking my life and maybe yours, too, that I can make them believe me."

I believed this last of what he was saying, about the rest I wasn't sure. "If I'm so powerful," I asked, "why did I let myself be taken so easily?"

"You are powerful, but you are also humble. You display your power only if sufficiently provoked."

He had answers, but answers weren't enough. He had also to be convincing and he wasn't convincing me.

"The earth moved," I said. "From the way you talk it's not a natural phenomenon. What is it? A leftover war weapon? We were a survival training station. We had no weapons development units aboard."

Again I thought I saw his mental wheels

turning. "No," he said, not looking at me. I could hardly hear him, he was keeping his voice so low. We were almost at the edge of the center square. "Not a war weapon. More a tool."

I'd already guessed he didn't like being pushed, but I had to know. "Not good enough," I said. "What is it?"

"Inside," he said roughly, shoving me toward the long house and the gathering chiefs. At the sound of his voice a head turned in our direction but for once he gave it no notice. "It was supposed to be the ultimate answer to the problem of wartime matériel and supply but as you can see, the side effect isn't what they expected. Now inside," and the measure of his desperation broke through for me when I heard him add, "please."

CHAPTER 9

For whatever effect it might have on the gathered conclave of chiefs, I sat quietly on my pad, my legs crossed, a wrist on either knee. It was the position I'd taken on this dais after I'd beaten Hagor and unwittingly sealed their champion's doom. Except that I wasn't wrapping myself in any metal cocoon of warmth. I was listening to Sten and watching him waving his arms and pointing to me with his wand and I wasn't liking what I was hearing and seeing.

I didn't know what he was saying, but the chiefs crowding the room did and their faces under their flat fur hats were translation enough. I guessed these men were far from being awed by any threat of displeasure from me coming from Sten. What I read in their eyes turning to me was resentment and a re-directed guilt. Among them were the men who had pushed Hagor forward for what they felt would be sport and could not now admit to themselves that they were to blame for what had happened to him.

These were not men to threaten, particu-larly not with me, and Sten should have known that. Perhaps the clan tradition was right and his contact with the outsiders' lan-guage had indeed warped his thinking, clouded his perception of his own people.

If I needed more to tell me that Sten was a man in dire trouble with those he sought to convince, I had only to look over their heads at those of the villagers who'd managed to crowd themself in after the chiefs, Meta tall among them.

I could see it in the way Uldhaar sat on his drum, his face unworried and faintly smiling. Somewhere in the dim past a man who under-stood these things had said "give me six words out of a man's mouth and I will use them to hang him" and the chief of chiefs looked to be letting his jester, his shaman, whatever Sten was, do just that.

Sten was hanging himself with the torrent pouring from his mouth and, from the urgent note of deperation I heard creeping into his voice, I think he knew he'd made his play and lost, and hung himself and maybe me, too. But still he couldn't seem to stop what by now was clearly a hopeless harangue.

I sensed the chiefs had suddenly grown ex-pectant. I looked at Uldhaar. The smile was gone from his face. The time had come to chop Sten down and maybe me with him. Sten had given him the chance to rid himself of his challenge once and for all, and Uldhaar did not mean to let it slip away. He rubbed his palms along his legs and started to get up.

I beat him to it. I stood up, stretched out my arms over my head as I had on the dais and this time had their attention at once.

Theirs and Sten's. He turned in mid-gesture to stare at me. I walked slowly, not too slowly, to him and put a hand on his head, holding the other high. Uldhaar had made it to his feet, he had only to call out and I'd be gone.

My hand on Sten's head, I spoke to him without moving my lips. "Tell them I'm putting my words into your mouth with my touch. Tell them."

He closed his eyes and took a long time answering. I took the time to stare over his head and count my heartbeats. Count them and wonder how desperate and how smart he would be. How desperate and how smart *I* was being.

When he opened his eyes, I saw a man who'd read the chiefs' faces perhaps better than I and was as much at a loss as to what to do to save himself from what he now knew was the monumental, the fatal, blunder he'd made in flatly challenging Uldhaar's authority. He nodded once, curtly.

I took my hand away and he faced his people, spoke to them rapidly in their tongue, his voice to my ears as hoarse with his tension as with the sounds of the language.

"Tell them," I said, "to do as you wish in the matter of the shaking earth. Tell them I am losing patience with you. I am losing patience with them all."

His eyes were wide on mine. It was more or less what he'd just tried to put across and hung himself in the trying.

"Tell them." I said and he did, but his voice was flat, he wasn't believing his own words. If I was to pull anything back from the brink to which he'd brought us, I knew I would have to do it alone.

I turned and faced the chiefs, the villagers, glanced at Uldhaar dropped back onto his drum. I raised my arms and spoke to them directly. Sten would repeat to them, what I said, he had no other choice, but I would be looking into their eyes.

"Two men." I said. "Two of your most powerful men, come forward."

Silence, then a murmur, a shuffling of feet met Sten's words repeating my challenge, but no one came forward to accept it.

"Two men who are confident in their strength, who do not fear to test it against me, against my power. Surely there are two such among you,"

I meant to sound disparaging and if they didn't hear the tone in Sten's voice, they caught it in mine. They were crowding in closer, faces were reddening, here and there one man pushed another.

Against the wall the villagers were looking

at each other and at their chiefs with uncertain faces. Still no one moved forward. The chiefs, the villagers, all were silent.

Behind me Uldhaar barked a command. I did not turn to look at him. My eyes were on the assembled men. I did not look to Sten for explanation. It would come soon enough and the silence was deepening.

Uldhaar was suddenly beside me, pointing at one man and then another, both powerful looking men, bellowing at them in a voice that brooked no disobedience, no hesitation.

But they did hesitate. Then first one, and then the other, shucked off their cloaks and came to stand in front of me. Uldhaar said something to them that I did not understand, but I saw them look at each other and flex their fingers and lick their lips before their faces set into slit-eyed masks of determination.

I pointed to one. "Tell him," I said to Sten. "to put his hands on my middle and when I give the signal, to lift me. Tell him he will do it easily."

Sten looked as uncertain as the man to whom he was repeating my instructions but the man moved in.

I put one hand on his shoulder as if to steady myself and, when I felt his grip firm on my waist, I gestured upward with the other.

He lifted me. A yard up off my feet and it was well that I had firm hold of his shoulder else he would have flung me back across my pad to smash against the far wall of the hut.

As it was, I landed hard on my feet, the jarring shock an unpleasant reminder of the depth of the menace arrayed against me.

I beckoned to the second man, the more powerful looking of the two. He repeated the performance except that this time I was prepared and landed lightly on my feet. I looked over to where Uldhaar sat, read nothing in his face. I could only guess at what he'd said to his men.

I shifted my eyes to Sten. He looked thoroughly puzzled by what he was seeing. I hoped the others shared his confusion.

I pointed to the first chief, the one who had tried to fling me across the hut. "You who choose to flaunt your strength. I take it from you with a wave of my hand. Your arms are now as those of a boy, your body as that of a weak woman. Come, flaunt your power on me now. If you can."

I spoke directly to him, but not looking at him. I was being as casual as the flip of my hand, leaving it to Sten to repeat my words.

He did, his voice as uncertain as the chief's eyes were determined. The man moved in. I put my hand on his shoulder as before, except that now it was extended and rigid. I signaled with my free hand and again he tried to grip me by my waist and lift.

He tried. He'd get me up on my toes and I'd fall back. He'd spread his legs and try to settle himself and couldn't. My arm, stiff on his shoulder, was keeping him from closing the gap between us, from planting himself solidly under me. Atlas would have had a problem lifting at arm's length two hundred Earth pounds that kept shifting away from him as he struggled to close in for the needed leverage.

I did not keep it up. It was enough that I show him trying and failing. Failing, red-faced, more from frustration than exertion, but red-faced.

I stepped away from him and turned to the second man. He was sharper than his clansman. He had hold of me almost before I'd finished the movement and for an instant I felt dismay. Then I put my hand high on his shoulder, feeling with my thumb for the carotid artery that pulsed in his neck.

I pressed. Not sharply, but gently, firmly. I did not look at him but turned my head to Uldhaar as if awaiting a signal from him.

It took Uldhaar a moment, but he nodded. He'd been staring all the while, but I thought he looked pleased at my show of deference to his authority.

My reason for looking in his direction had been not to curry his favor, but because of the firm hold his chief had on my waist. This man was set to throw me against the hut's low ceiling the moment I gave him the signal to lift. I had to escape.

I returned Uldhaar's nod slowly. I was stalling for time. Stalling until, from the corner of my eye I saw with relief the chief who held me shake his head as if to clear it, felt his grip loosen momentarily, but enough.

I slid my hand down his shoulder and stepped away, my arm rigid. I'd been cutting

blood off from his brain with my thumb. That
Uldhaar thought otherwise was an unexpected plus. And it sparked a plan in my groping brain. A plan of which I doubted Sten
would approve. I looked about for Meta. She
was still at the back of the hut. I would need
her.

I finished off the second man as readily as
I had the first. Had I been working a less
deadly game I might have taken a moment to
savor the almost comical dismay mirrored in
their faces. As it was, I dared not risk their
discovering that their helplessness was an illusion any more than I had with their fallen
champion. That they, like Hagor, were victims of a stage magician's trick.

I waved my hand as I had before. "Enough,"
I said. "I give you back your strength and
more. Come, prove it for yourselves."

I turned to Uldhaar, my hand partly raised,
my look questioning.

He understood my gesture. He nodded his
permission even before Sten repeated my
words. It was well that he did, I was not yet
finished.

I held a forefinger up to the crowd. "One
finger. You have seen how at the wave of my
hand the strength of your chiefs deserts them
and they become as children." I raised my
finger higher. "See now how I give them in
one finger such power as each had in the
whole of his body. See and marvel."

I may have sounded stentorian, I meant to.
I waited until Sten had finished repeating my
words before I beckoned him closer. He'd

looked no less puzzled, but his voice was firmer.

"Tell your clansmen to each show one finger to the crowd," I said. "Tell them to show it well so that all may see. Tell them to then place the finger under my instep, one on each side, and when I say the word "now" to lift. Tell them they will raise me up easily. They have the power. They have heard me say so and they believe."

The chiefs did as they were told, almost eagerly. Shaken, looking at Uldhaar and licking their lips as they waited for my signal.

I stood, my arms ostensibly outstretched for balance and obviously having trouble. I beckoned Sten to stand in front of me and steadied myself with a hand on each of his shoulders.

I nodded. "Now," I said and the chiefs lifted. Motivation is a wonderful thing, there are some who claim it is the only thing. I do not, but I felt myself go up, heard the gasps of relief from the chiefs, saw it almost as a glow in their faces. Even if I hadn't helped with my pressure on Sten's shoulders, two hundred pounds is only a hundred each and what is that to a man who in the core of his being needs badly to believe.

It had happened as I said it would, their strength returned and in full measure and more. What they did before with both hands, they now appeared to have accomplished each with but a finger. I was sure that for a while their mind-set would be such that they would indeed display more power. It might

stay with them, it might with time ebb away.
It was no matter. For now and in this moment
they were believers.

I swept my eyes out over the gathered
clansmen, looking for the skeptics, counting
the believers.

I looked at Sten. He was among the skeptics, clearly. Or maybe he'd figured out by
now that I wasn't playing to the chiefs, but to
Uldhaar and didn't like where that left him. I
hadn't expected he would. That was why I
needed Meta.

Last of all I looked at Uldhaar. I would not
have lightly played poker with the chief of
chiefs. I strode across the space between us.
The two guards he'd detailed to be with me
at all times had returned. Now they moved to
place themselves between me and Uldhaar.
After what they'd seen me do to the two
chiefs, it took courage and a devotion it
pleased me to see.

I held up my hands, palms forward to show
them I meant no harm to Uldhaar and smiled
when they flinched. Sten had not moved to
follow me. He'd turned back to the chiefs and
I guessed that after the display I'd just put on,
he felt his argument was back on track. I
couldn't blame him if he sounded bombastic.
He was taking a shot at deposing with words
and the threat to unleash a sorcerer a man
who wore two swords and carried hidden a
dagger capable of piercing armor.

Except that I wasn't a sorcerer and I had little trust in a man who would talk himself to

power saying that I was. I had little trust in any man who would seize power, period.

I had some seizing to do myself, like an initiative to get me free of this hidden people. Yet if what Sten had said to me about the earthquakes and a war tool gone awry was true, I'd be literally escaping from a grand-daddy of a story. And adding to the gnawing was the dazzling speed I'd seen of the animals these clansmen ran and rode. I'd traveled across the stars on the trail of one story; if I managed to escape, I'd be running from two.

Around the hut's one low room, sitting hunched down on their heels or standing shoulder to shoulder against the walls, were close-packed chiefs and villagers. I walked out among them. I sensed Uldhaar's guards behind me.

I stopped before a face I knew, not that of a chief. It was Crossbow, one of the two who'd brought me in and laughed at my discomfiture in the snow. I motioned him to his feet, looked at him long as if considering. Apprehension was plain in the eyes he kept fixed somewhere past my shoulder. I shook my head and moved on. His relief was audible.

I stopped before another and still another. Their relief when I moved on was as plain to hear as Crossbow's. In the silence that hung in the room, Sten's voice, hoarse with his language and his effort to regain his people's attention, was only a counterpoint. I was making my way gradually toward the wall

against which I saw Meta standing and he
may have divined my attention.

I stopped before a woman now, and another, and then I was facing Meta, her expression sullen and at the same time
uncertain. I took the time to look at her as
long as I had the others before I put my hand
on her head. It was what I'd done with Sten
to give excuse to his ability to understand and
repeat my words. But to Meta I spoke openly.

"You can admit you know Galactic, or I can
keep making Sten look good. For how much
longer I don't know. But he's not going to
make it and I think you know it."

She did know, but it was plain she didn't
like hearing me tell her. I saw her eyes grow
more sullen. She didn't look like the others
of the clan, she looked like the sister Claire
Morgan denied she had.

I spoke quickly. "Don't be a complete fool,
Meta. You're as much a prisoner here as I am.
I don't know what Sten's promised you, but
look at him, take a good look. Do you still
think he can get you out?"

Her eyes moved to Sten, narrowed. She said
nothing, but she jerked her head out from under my hand. Heads were turned to look at
us. No one was listening to Sten.

"Suit yourself," I said. "Trust him if you
like." I took her by an arm. She could still
bolt and I would not go after her. "Come with
me," I said. I had to talk to Uldhaar and talk
to him before his chiefs could scatter and
while some awe of me still clung to their
minds. "I need a mouthpiece and you're it.

And remember," I added, "right now Sten looks credible because of what I just did. You think to tear me down, you tear him down as well." I was cautioning her, but I had the feeling that it was I who needed to be on guard as well.

I made my way back to my pad without looking to see if she was following me and sat down. The only ones seated in the yurtlike hut were Uldhaar and myself. He on his drum, I cross-legged on my pad. The two guards stood behind me, Meta hesitated, then moved up to one side between the chief and me. The lesser chiefs would stay squatting, standing, until Uldhaar signaled them permission to leave.

I looked at Sten absently rolling his wand between his palms, but I spoke to Meta. "My compliments to the chief of chiefs, and ask him how he enjoyed my performance."

I chose the word performance deliberately and when I saw Sten's eyes narrow and his wand motion stop, I knew my instinct not to let him translate my words to Uldhaar had been right.

Meta was silent, her eyes on Sten. "Forget Sten," I snapped at her. "His way is dead. Tell Uldhaar what I said. Tell him exactly."

At my mention of his name, Uldhaar looked up at Meta, his waiting for her to translate plain. Her eyes darted about, then settled on me. I saw her tongue lick at the lips that were twin to Claudia's before she spoke in a low voice, the hoarse language sounding breathy coming from her.

Sten had heard what I'd said to Meta, he knew what she was saying to Uldhaar. I watched his face intently for any quick widening of his eyes, any fleeting expression that would tell me that she was putting her own twist on my words. I saw none. It was a scanty testing, but I dared risk no more.

I looked up at my two guards leaning in, saw the interest sparking in their eyes. What I meant to reveal to Uldhaar I did not want spread among the clan.

"What I have to say is for Uldhaar's ears alone. Could he tell his men to stand away?" This time Meta did not look to Sten for guidance before she translated my words in her breathy voice.

Uldhaar barked an order and the two guards stepped back and well away. So did Sten, color washing into his face.

I let him go. It was just as well that he stay as much in the dark as the others.

Uldhaar motioned Meta to a place between us. She knelt and sat back on her long legs. The sullen look was melting from her dark eyes, her gaze shifting from me to Uldhaar and back again.

I spoke to her. "I said what I did was a performance. Did Uldhaar understand that?"

She translated swiftly and gave me his answer, "Yes."

It was the first word of Galactic I'd heard her speak. The breathy tone seemed to be natural to her. "Good," I said. It was time to be specific.

I was. I went over my performance with the

two chiefs, explaining what it was I had done, the principles underlying the effects he had just witnessed. I did not go back to Hagor. That was a sobering memory and trickery only in part.

Perhaps I went into greater detail than was necessary, but I can resist an appreciative listener no better than any other human. Uldhaar laughed and slapped his thigh and had me repeat what I'd said when Meta's explanation was not clear to him.

The clan chiefs looks at one another, their faces uncertain. I don't think they expected Uldhaar to respond with laughter to anything I had to say and it was making them nervous. Had I cast a spell over their head man? Sten had called me sorcerer and while they had no feeling for the occult, they had seen what they had seen. One chief started to get to his feet only to be pulled down by his companions on either side. Someone tittered.

"I would respectfully suggest to the chief of chiefs that he not speak of these secrets to his people. It would only make his men feel foolish in the eyes of their comrades. I reveal them to him only to show I have no occult powers, that I have no wish to deceive."

Meta translated my words and Uldhaar's answer. "He takes your point," she said. "And he agrees with the wisdom of your suggestion."

I nodded and added a caution for her. "You might also keep what we say to yourself, Meta. Nobody likes a gabby translator." And when she fixed me with her eyes, I reminded

her that the head man might get upset with her
if she were to go spreading about what he'd
already decided was better kept quiet.

I felt the ground under me sway, the skin
walls of the hut on their lattice framework
swaying with it. I didn't need the reminder.
The muttering of the chiefs was apprehen-
sive and, if Sten was to be believed, justifi-
ably so.

I leaned forward, I did not need to fake the
urgency in my voice. "You saw me rob your
men of their strength, you now know it was
not real but illusion."

I waited until I saw him nod his answer to
Meta's words before I went on.

"This shaking of the ground is no illusion,
but it is not real. It is not an earthquake as
you know earthquakes."

From the sharp way he looked at me, his
brows beetling, I did not need Meta to tell me
what he'd said to know I was on shaky ground
in more ways than one. I did not know if Sten
had the interest of his planet at heart in fighting Uldhaar, or if he was out to depose him
and the earthquake had handed him a con-
venient excuse. I did not even know for certain if I ought to take Sten's words that it was
not a natural phenomenon.

What I did know was that I was not looking
to be kingmaker for Sten or anyone else.
What I wanted was out and I wanted the story
if there was one. But to achieve either, I
needed first to convince Uldhaar that he
owed it to his people to check out the possi-
bility that Sten might be right about the im-

minent danger to them and to his world. I had to convince him in spite of his unwillingness to go against a traditional explanation about something I was sure he'd heard from Sten and already set his mind not to accept.

I meant to begin with what I'd shown him with his chiefs as an illustration and segue as I could from it to the earthquakes. If I was lucky, I might get him to agree to at least allow Sten or someone to look into what might be causing them.

I leaned forward, braced for an uphill struggle. "Your men seemed to grow weak and all were certain I was the cause of it. You now know I was not. In the same way, might not what makes the earth move under our feet be other than what it seems?"

Uldhaar shot a single word at Meta that surprised me. "True," she translated, her voice sounding a little startled.

He'd spoken almost before she'd finished with what I had said and I started to get the feeling that Uldhaar might well have his own thoughts about what made the earth move. That it was not blind tradition that was holding him hidebound, but the sticky fact that the call for action was being put to him as a demand by someone who would use it to contest his leadership.

I did not feel it unreasonable to surmise that the severity of the earthquake that had sparked Sten to premature action may also have jarred Uldhaar to deciding he must to find a way around Sten and quickly—and I could be it.

I could provide a way for Uldhaar to do what urgently needed to be done without it looking as though he was capitulating to Sten's demands.

The earth stirred, lightly, but it stirred. I took the plunge. "Your chiefs are getting restless," I said. I spoke directly to Uldhaar. "Send them home."

Beside me Meta gasped audibly. I smiled at her. "Tell him," I said. I appreciated her quandary. I suppose few people tell a clan chief what to do and I wasn't. I was calling his attention to the obvious. "Tell him." I said again.

She licked her lips and interpreted what I'd said, speaking as though she expected a physical blow to chop off her words.

Uldhaar looked at me and I looked at Uldhaar. Presently he raised his voice and the chiefs began to file out of the hut, some looking back at Sten, but only a few. When the last of them but two I took to be Uldhaar's personal attendants were gone, he directed his attention and his voice at the two guards and then at Sten.

The two guards moved in until they again stood over me, but their eyes had a different look. Sten's face went white and then red. He looked ready to pop an artery.

"What's going on?" I asked Meta.

"Wait and see," she snapped at me. She looked as put out by what Uldhaar was saying as Sten. In my head I heard the sound of applecarts turning over.

Uldhaar stood up, clapped me on the shoul-

der, and fired words at Meta. She passed them
to me with ill grace. "You are a man of great
wisdom. Uldhaar puts in your hands the matter of the moving earth. He gives you the two
guards and Sten to assist you as you may need
them, and you are free to go about his domain as you wish."

I looked at Uldhaar in silent appreciation.
He wore the skins of animals and carried
bladed weapons, but there was nothing primitive about the workings of his mind. In one
sweep the earthquakes would be checked
out. The two guards would still be on me, but
assigning them to me as helpers chopped Sten
down to an assistant and but one of three at
that. And the chief was rid of what to do
about me.

"Thank Uldhaar, chief of chiefs, for his
generous expression of trust," I said, "and
ask him if I may let his jester, Sten, keep his
knowledge of my language?"

Uldhaar listened, looked at me, and chuck-
led. "Of course," Meta said, and I wondered
just how secret Sten's secret was, or if it was
my use of the word jester that amused the
chief.

I waited until Uldhaar and his two attendant chiefs were gone before I turned to Sten.
"All right," I said. "I've got the head man's
okay to do what needs to be done. Now what
is it about the ground shaking that has you so
worked up?"

But Meta was on him ahead of me. "You
fool. If you had any real brains you would

have known better than to try to frighten Uldhaar with a would-be wizard."

I caught the would-be and thought for the moment she was going to spill the rest of what she'd heard me tell Uldhaar.

"Stop screaming, Meta." Under cover of his body, Sten jerked a thumb at the two guards, who were looking at her with more than curiosity, but she ignored his gesture of warning.

"I was doing all right until I let you talk me into going along with you on your stupid power play."

"You were doing all right? Uldhaar wouldn't even talk to you. It was you who came to me, remember?"

"I only came to you for help in getting to see him. I didn't think you'd want me to help you take over the clans."

"There is no other way. He's paranoid about somebody finding out that we exist. Did you think you could have talked him into letting you walk away with even one of his beasts?"

"Beasts?" I cut in. "What beasts?"

"Never mind," Sten brushed me aside. He was still pointing to the guards, in close and beginning to smirk. "If you don't quiet down, Meta, I'm going to have to hit you."

Her eyes narrowed. She was a head and more taller than he. "Go ahead, I'll even give you first swing."

"Stop it, Meta," I said. "You, Sten, your performance persuading the chiefs was less than brilliant, do you want to come out second best in a brawl with a woman, too?"

I don't know if it was the good sense of what I said or the insult, but he quieted down. "You felt the ground, Meta. The planet destructs, where are you and your beasts then? We've had a setback, but that's all it is, a setback. I can still muster support."

"Hold it," I said. If the planet was in danger of being destroyed, I'd do what I could to help him on that. Other considerations aside, there was the story to be gotten. Of that and of the beasts about which he'd snapped at Meta. But if Sten had the delusion that he could still ride to the top on my back, it was just that, a delusion.

"Hold it, Sten. If you want to hassle with Uldhaar, you do it on your own. Later. Right now there are the earthquakes you were hot to stop. I'm in charge and, like it or not, that's the way it is. Now, what do we do?" I figured that, except for his not being in charge, he had a plan worked out.

Sten didn't answer. His eyes wandered around the hut, rested a moment on the two old women tending the fire at its center, followed the thin wisp of the smoke rising to escape out the hole in the roof. He looked everywhere but at me.

I started to get an uneasy feeling that I was wrong about him having a plan, that Sten was better at talking than at doing, more mouth than real brains. "You don't know," I said. I was at once aghast and reconciled. "Beyond getting control of the clan, you really don't know what to do, do you?"

His silence was answer enough. I stared at him. What did he have to be resentful about?

I turned to Meta. "What did you. . . ?"

The ground shook. A sickening lurch that were the hut more solidly built would have brought the structure down. As it was, the lattice framework creaked in a way it had not done before and a section of the roof broke free to fall against the fire. One of the old women let out a shriek as a burning ember flew out to strike her on her foot.

One of the guards yelled something at Sten. Sten yelled back, and the two men glared at each other.

I looked at Meta. "The same thing you asked him," she said. "He wants to know what Sten is going to do about the earth moving." Her lips curled. "He made a lot of promises it looks like he doesn't know how to keep."

"He won't have to now," I said. "Uldhaar put me in charge."

"Yes, he did, didn't he? Then it's you who'd better come up with an answer." She laughed, a nasty sound. "These people have an attitude about losers. Maybe you noticed."

I thought of Hagor, heard his scream again. "I noticed," I said. "I noticed."

CHAPTER 10

"You're not being much help, Sten," I said. "From the noises you've been making, I expected you to know more about this thing you called a tool gone wrong than I seem to be able to pull out of you."

If he was as short on facts as he seemed to want me to believe, he would not be the first seeker of power I'd come across who sounded better than he actually was. But he could still be looking to topple Uldhaar, and so was telling me as little as he could.

"I appreciate your dilemma," I said. "If you help me and we save *Thul*, I look good and Uldhaar looks good for putting me in charge. If you hold back and your planet goes, what does that leave for you to be head man of? Where does that leave you, period?"

I could appreciate his dilemma, but I didn't intend to pander to it. He could balance his hunger for power against the need of his planet on his own.

Uldhaar had assigned the two guards to be my assistants and maybe they were. But when I sat down to talk to Sten and had Meta tell them they needn't stand by, that I would call them when I needed them, they smiled and nodded and stayed where they were. If I had any thought that I could escape Uldhaar's hospitality with a story or without it, that settled it for me.

I turned to Meta. "You're not one of Sten's people, that's plain enough. What did he tell you to suck you into this flopped power play of his?"

She'd called him a fool. I was hoping she would now see him as one dangerously blind to reality as well.

Meta looked from Sten to me to Sten and back again to me. Then she got interested in the condition of her fingernails.

I stood up. "I'm in no mood to coax you, Meta. I don't know what it is you hope you can hold me up for, but you're not in what I'd call an enviable position from which to bargain." I looked down at Sten. "Neither of you are."

I beckoned to my guard helpers, headed for the door. With any kind of an opener, I would have done what I could to save the planet and get my story. Without it, I could still try to save my own neck. I wanted another look at the animal pens.

Under me the ground trembled, only slightly. Sten's voice came after me. "Pike!"

I hadn't liked being made to coax, I didn't make him grovel. I went back to my pad, sat down, the guards following me faithfully.

"Talk," I said.

"I . . . I hardly know where to begin."

"Stop stalling, Sten. How about telling me what this tool is. How is it going to split the planet? If it's a wartime thing, how come I never heard of it when I was stationed here?"

The answer to this last was simple. I'd never heard of it because I wasn't supposed to. Camouflage can be worked on an idea as well as on a thing. The military tank had appeared, even got its name, on the drawing board not as the war machine it actually was, but as an innocent mobile field water tank.

"It was a tool, is a tool. But when we got to setting up a working prototype, we found things happening we didn't anticipate. We were still working on it when the Peace Action ended and the project was abandoned. Or it was supposed to be. From the way the earth is moving, somebody resurrected it."

"If you thought it so much a danger, why didn't you just go out and stop what needed to be stopped? Why did you even mention it to Uldhaar?"

"I . . . I don't know what it looks like, and I don't know where it is. It's mobile. I needed the hunters to help me find it, but to Uldhaar an earthquake was an earthquake. He wouldn't give the order to search."

"I can see why," I said. "Especially after you

tried to lean on him. But you don't know what it looks like? You said you worked on it."

"I did, on parts of it, I never saw the whole of it assembled."

"So you figured to depose Uldhaar and give the order yourself."

Sten nodded, and I believed that was the way it was for him at the start. Except when he saw the potential of the power he was trying to wrest from Uldhaar, the concept got away from him.

"You said it was a tool," I prompted him. "To do what?"

He took a deep breath. "Mining. Matrix mining."

Matrix mining? I'd never heard of it. I told Sten so.

"The Peace Action was using up essential materials and the pace was growing. Suppliers were getting tougher and tougher to negotiate with. Transporter beams were already in use, so someone suggested a way might be worked out for a ship to stand off-planet and transport what was needed directly out of the earth without bothering the planet's inhabitants."

"You mean steal what you wanted out from under them without them being any the wiser."

"Payment was up to the negotiators. Our problem was the machine."

Sten spoke Galactic, but he also wore animal skins and lived in a skin yurt. I didn't see him contributing to what had to be a sophisticated piece of equipment.

"How did you get to work on this . . . this super mining probe?"

Sten looked suddenly discomfited, "They needed to keep the project undercover. To avoid talk, they hired people who didn't speak Galactic. They could talk among themselves, maybe, but not to outsiders. It worked. You said you never heard of the project."

So Sten had been a grunt. A smart grunt who took advantage of the opportunity to learn the Galactic English he heard the green-coated lab types speaking.

But a transporter beam needed a terminal at both ends, had they found a way around that? And what was a mining matrix?

The matrix was just that. A force field in which were embedded the subatomic codes of elements to match those of whatever it was they were after. The transporter beam kept both its terminals. With a variation. They were set side by side and the beam, emanating from one, passed through the matrix, bounced off the target and came back to the other, bringing with it bits of the target structure to match the programming matrix.

"I take it the basic concept worked. What was the problem you didn't anticipate?"

"Problems. More than one and they compounded. The matrix. Control wasn't complete. The beam picked up what it was told to, but also anything that came close to the matrix pattern."

"So you had impurities. You get those with any ore."

"The impurities weren't the problem," Sten

said. "Look, did you ever put your hand in a bucket of water and yank it out suddenly? Did you notice how the water rushed in to fill the space where your hand had been?"

"Not that I remember," I said, "but I can see what you mean."

"That's what happened with the atoms the beam yanked out. Whatever was around them sagged into the empty space."

"And that makes the earth shake. So if your beam took bigger bites than you at first thought it would, set it to take smaller ones and space them farther apart."

But even the greediest of renegades taking the biggest of bites would have a long way to go to chew up a planet the size of *Thul*. And certainly not all that speedily. What had pressed Sten to make him rush into trying his failed power play when he did? I asked him.

"It's not the bite itself," he said. "It's the vibrations it sets up. Every so often you get one that reverberates. Sets up a series of echo waves that reflect back and forth and overlap and build. If they ever hit the synchronization just right, the whole planet goes. Like a snapped glass, the whole planet goes." His voice was going up.

"Don't get excited," I said. "We'll find your transporter. Where do we start?"

"I don't know, it's a sizable unit, at least the one I worked on was, but it was built to be mobile. It could be anywhere. That's why I needed the hunters."

I looked at the two guards. They'd taken to playing some sort of finger game.

"You can forget fanning out hunters," I said. "We've got two men, maybe four more if they don't stop rotating the shifts, and that's it. If Uldhaar meant to give me the all-out support you wanted from him, he'd have done so. I don't think he feels a need for urgency."

I thought of Baran and Claire and my camera. He, too, had been searching for a unit that he'd worked on that was mobile and that was valuable enough to pay the cost of coming to *Thul* to find it. It might be Sten's transporter, or it might not be.

My record camera was in its pocket on my sleeve, but it had no infrared capability. But then I hadn't seen any particularly hot spots on my larger one's screen when Baran had shouted in my ear.

"This matrix mining machine, does it give off much heat?"

Sten was ahead of me. "None that you can pick up at any distance. Actually, it absorbs energy from its surroundings. Icing up was another of the problems."

It absorbed energy! Baran had been looking over my shoulder not for hot spots, but for one colder than the area around it. The dark fan shape at the corner of my screen he'd had me zoom in on! The screen of my camera Claire had taken from me when she dumped me out to die in the cold.

I looked at the helpers I knew were my guards. I looked at Sten. I looked at Meta. "How do I find your sister?" I said.

Meta looked at me. "I don't have a sister," she said.

Right now I had neither the time nor the inclination to brace Meta about Claire. I turned to Sten. "Ask my guards if they know the way into town."

Back in my service days, they issued me something called a Government Property Pass. We carried around a great deal of photo gear. Mixed. Cameras, printers, holo projectors, power packs. It was all government property, much of it forbidden to other ratings and civilians alike, so we had to have chits to show it was all right for us Photo Mates to have it. It meant a separate chit for each separate piece, and what do you do about accessories and cables and other odd bits?

It was all pretty unwieldy until a clear-thinking Photo Lab C.O. issued his photographers a blanket pass. One government property pass to cover all the pieces of government photo property his men had the need and the right to carry.

The key words were "Government Property" and "Pass." It didn't take long to discover that transport pool personnel considered the vehicles in their charge government property as well and would yield up a scooter or a skimmer to a burdened photo mate on the mere presentation of his "Government Property Pass." With a little imagination and fast talk, it would also get you past an MP guarding a base gate.

The guard would stop you and you would flash your pass. "That's not a liberty pass," he or she would point out.

"Of course not. It's a government property

pass. The base is government property, isn't it?"

The guard's eyes would cross a little and he—or she—would wave you through. Which of them was going to risk bothering a superior to check you out when what you had was plainly a government property pass and the base was undeniably government property.

My beard that I'd been letting grow to shield my face from *Thul's* cold was scrawny but fuller. I didn't know where Claire or Baran might have my camera, but with a snow visor, my fur hat, and an animal skin cloak, I might be able to get close enough to one or the other of them to do something about getting it back before she or he recognized me.

"What are you going to do?" Sten wanted to know. "Your guards won't take you anywhere near town. Uldhaar has given them orders."

"If I'm to locate your matrix miner, I need my camera." I told him about Claire Morgan and Baran. I noticed Meta was listening as closely as he.

I nodded at the two guards, "Uldhaar's orders are for them to help me as I need them. Ask."

The two guards answered Sten with blank faces. They would not even admit to knowing the town existed.

Domain was a word as subject to interpretation as "Government Property."

"Look at each other," I said. "Which one of you is willing to go to his chief of chiefs and say to him that there are reaches of his domain whose existence you do not recognize?"

They looked at each other, but only glancingly, from the corners of their eyes.

"Is not the whole of the planet *Thul* the domain of Uldhaar? I ask you again. Which of you will tell him it is not?"

The two men were still not meeting each other's eyes.

"They won't admit it, even if they know." Sten interjected. I quieted him with a gesture of my hand, stood waiting.

The taller guard broke. He licked his lips and nodded.

"Fine," I said. "Tell him to come with me. Tell his friend to stay with you."

Sten didn't interpret my words to them. "He won't go alone," he said to me. "They always travel in pairs."

"We will be a pair, he and I. Tell them."

"I'll go with you."

I grinned at Sten. "You can't. You don't have the freedom of Uldhaar's domain. I do. Tell them."

Sten had no answer for me but he wasn't ready to quit. "You'll need an interpreter. Take Meta, then."

That thought had crossed my mind, but it died even as it was being born. I didn't need Meta along to scream away my cover the moment she set eyes on Claire, deny her sister though she had.

"I'll manage. Tell the guards."

Sten looked disgruntled, but he passed what I'd said on to my guards. I tried to watch Meta's eyes as he did so for any sign that he was adding a note of his own, but she hid them from me, keeping her gaze turned down on her hands in her lap.

The guards looked uncertain, then they moved apart, one going to stand behind Sten. I hoped he took my instructions to mean he was to keep as tight a watch on Sten as I expected Uldhaar had ordered him to keep on me.

I pointed to the guard who was to be my guide. Smooth faced, taller than his companion, but still coming barely up to my shoulder. "What is your name?" I said.

"Kort," the man said, looking not at Sten, who'd repeated my question, but at me. It was a good sign.

"Kort. I am called Pike," and I held out my hand.

I'd noticed that these men did not have the custom of shaking hands, but it was time this one started thinking of me in a way other than orthodox.

He stared at my outstretched hand, then lifted puzzled eyes up to mine. I reached out, took his hand, and shook it. He looked pleased. I caught the look he shot at his friend behind Sten and went around and took his hand as well. If it pleased one, it might please the other. I could use all the good will I could get.

"Pike," I said. "My name is Pike."

"Rhyf," he said without my asking and looked as pleased as his taller friend. It crossed my mind that maybe he was the one I should be taking to town with me, except that he didn't know the way. And then it occurred to me that maybe he did, but was sharp enough not to have stuck out his neck by admitting it. Maybe that made him the right one to guard Sten.

I pointed to Sten, I pointed to Meta, and I pointed to the ground. "You and Meta stay here," I said and saw Rhyf nod. I hoped Kort was as sharp as he in picking up on my signing.

Or maybe they both knew more Galactic than either was willing to let on. You can tell your young people, you can order them not to, but how can you *make* them, and what is the harm if they do touch with the outside, occasionally?

Sten was glaring at me with eyes that were wide with a growing anger. I guess the idea that I might be setting a watch on him did not sit well. "You're a fool," he said. "You won't make it off the planet even if you do manage to break away from your guard when you get to town. *If* you break away."

I laughed. "That's not my plan."

It wasn't. I wanted to find Sten's matrix miner, I wanted its story and maybe Meta's racing beast's as well. But most of all, I wanted my camera back. With it I was a journeyman photographer, without it I was a postwar drifter.

"Let's go," I said to Kort. "The stables first."

Sten spoke quickly to Kort, turning to include Rhyf, and it didn't sound like what I'd said. Meta stood up, thrust herself between the two men, Sten and Rhyf. She spat something in their hoarse tongue at Sten.

"Shut up," he said in Galactic.

She ignored him, not stopping what sounded a tirade in any language.

"Shut up," he said again and tried to put his hand over her mouth.

I reached out and caught his wrist, ground the bones between my fingers.

He yelped and sagged at the knees. I let go and he dropped the rest of the way.

"Do you want to tell me what this is all about?" I said to Meta.

"Claire will wipe you out."

I was pretty sure that wasn't what she'd been on Sten about. "I thought you said you didn't know Claire."

"I said I had no sister."

She was still in a spitting mode. She turned and ran past the two women who tended the fire and out the door of the hut. I let her go. I had no spare guard to send after her.

Sten was on his knees rubbing his wrist. If he wanted to look good, needed to look good to topple Uldhaar, I wasn't helping his image any.

"Let's go," I said again to Kort. "The stables first."

We were at the low, broad gate leading to the animal pens when I heard the whirring sound at my ear and instinctivly ducked away from it. I did not need to search the post next to my head to know what I would find, but I did. Someone among these sword-and-crossbow-carrying, skin-clad clansmen had just taken a shot at me with a thoroughly unprimitive needle gun.

CHAPTER 11

The afternoon was bright, an eye-tiring brightness even through the eyeslits of my sun visor. I had once been hunted on *Thul* by a bearlike carnivore the whiteness of whose coat kept me from seeing it against the snow until it was almost at the point of bringing me down. That feeling of a menace barely escaped was with me now as it had been with me then.

Whether by coincidence or Uldhaar's design to screen me from another shot at least until I was well away from his hidden valleys, I rode a *Thul* beast at the center of a group of his hunters. A small group, four hunters only, crossbowmen all, clad like myself in white pelts, they were to go with Kort and me until we were within skiing distance of Heyday and then to return, taking our mounts with them.

Their handsome pack of feline-looking snow animals ranged prettily out in front. All mature animals, no frolicking youngsters among them. Heads up, ears and eyes alert, different from my Earthside hounds, who had run in the main with their muzzles close to the ground. But then, *Thul*'s animals did not hunt by scent.

I would have taken pleasure in the sight, except that I was scanning the snow about me as diligently as they. The near-miss at the stables had unsettled more than me. Uldhaar had all but torn his huts apart searching for the weapon that had fired it. It has been said that in a kingdom of the blind, the man with one eye is king. In a community of swords and spears, much the same feeling might apply to a modern weapon.

He had not found it, but more than a score of his chiefs were now under guard by their fellows. The search had turned up stockpiles of weapons concealed from normal sight in double walls and hidden pits. The temper to break the constraints of ancient custom appeared to have been stronger than he, or even Sten, had suspected.

The gait of the *Thul* beast under me was not an altogether pleasant one. It did not alternate legs as did a horse, but moved both on the same side at the same time to give it a swaying motion which took some getting used to. Even at an easy lope, it was fast, faster than any saddle horse I'd ever ridden, but

I did not think it to be Harry Judd's racing beast. That, he'd said, could fly and while I did not doubt that the ill-tempered animal I rode could swim, I saw no way it could, Pegasus-like, fly.

A loud crunching underfoot broke in on my thinking. We were crossing a narrow chasm on a bridge of snow that sagged suddenly under our combined weight. It did not break away, but tilted so that two of the feline-looking pack animals closest to the edge slid over it and down.

I had a clear view of them going over and instinctively held my breath, waiting for the sound of their bodies dashing against the hard ice floor below.

It didn't happen.

Over the edge they went, their legs spread wide. I remembered the first of them I'd seen. The female sitting upright wrapped in a loose cloak of her own snowy pelt. Now I saw the pelt billow out on either side of the falling animals. Down they spiraled, like a pair of Earthside's flying squirrels. Down to land hard, but unhurt.

Beside me the hunters' language was strange, but what they said was not. The voices of men swearing at their ill luck.

Two rode back to more solid footing. One dismounted, took a coil of braided leather rope from his saddle, handed one end to his mounted companion, threw the other over the chasm lip and went down it hand over hand.

The rider's beast balked both times at haul-

ing up the two snow animals, but it obeyed
its rider's prodding. Their rescuer came up
the way he'd gone down, hand over hand. I
understood his not wanting to risk his companion's beast hauling him up as it had the
two animals that had fallen. Short of the
horses and cattle in old tapes of rodeo gath-
erings, these *Thul* beasts were more recalci-
trant than any I'd ever seen.

Twice more we stopped, rock still and flat,
while unsuspecting police vehicles swept past
in a flurry of whirling snow.

I settled myself on my skis and Kort and I
slid down the wall of the dish at the bottom
of which the shabby buildings of Heyday
huddled out of the wind. We came to a silent
stop under the window of my room on the
blind side of the hostel.

As we'd skied closer to town, the image of
a scraggly-bearded six footer wrapped in the
skin of an animal coming up on anyone un-
awares became more and more ludicrous in my
mind. I was glad now that at the last moment
of our hunter escort leaving us, I'd snatched
the coil of plaited leather rope from the pom-
mel of my saddle. I'd noticed the small grappling hook fixed to one end.

The window I'd cracked to get rid of the old
man's stew might still be unlocked. I whirled
the hook in a tight circle and flung it up toward the edge of the roof above. It caught on
the first attempt and I tested the line with my
weight. It held.

I went up the thin plait hand over hand. Not

as easily as I'd seen the rescuer of the fallen
snow animals do, but I went up. The window
was open and I slid it aside the rest of the way
and lifted myself over the sill. Kort made it
without even breathing hard.

I shucked off my cloak and went quietly
down the hall to listen outside Baran's door.
I heard nothing.

I tried the door. It was locked. My dirk
along the jamb might have gotten me inside,
but it would have left marks to warn Baran
and I did not want him alerted beforehand.

It was only the second day since he'd seen
what he wanted on my screen, he could be
coming back. He could have also checked out
and off the planet. I couldn't go down and ask
the old man. I couldn't go down and ask the
old man for his key to get inside either.

I went back to my room to wait. Baran
might not come, but I'd find that out soon
enough. It was better than lying on my stomach in the cold alongside the road ready to
waylay him on the way in.

Kort had been watching me from the partly
open door, his crossbow at the ready. A good
man, I thought, to cover me without my asking. Or maybe he had his orders from Uldhaar.

I left my door ajar and settled myself down
against the wall to wait. I did not want to pull
up a chair or lie down on the bed for fear the
old man would hear the creaking and come
up to check. I did not need to keep an eye to
the crack, the stairs would protest the weight
of a man even half a hundred pounds lighter

than Baran and warn me of his coming in plenty of time.

I waited. After a while I got stiff from not moving around. I got up and stretched. I pointed to my ear and down the hall and back to my ear. Kort nodded, and took my place alongside the door.

After a while he got up to stretch and I went back to listening. Then he spelled me and so on. We did that a few times while it got dark outside. The smell of the old man's stew coming up the stairs reminded me I hadn't had anything to eat since I gnawed on an animal leg early in the morning. My stomach rumbled at the thought.

The stew smell weakened and the rattle of eating coming up from downstairs died to silence and I finally admitted to myself that Baran wasn't going to show. The only lead I had been able to come up with was at a dead end. I'd helped Baran find what he was looking for and now he was gone.

I got to my feet. It was not what I wanted to do, but I hadn't eaten in a while and my chest pain was starting up. The sinking feeling in my stomach was not wholly due to hunger. I rubbed it, pointed to my mouth and then down to the floor, then back and forth to Kort and myself. We'd go down and eat. He nodded his understanding.

We'd eat and I'd get the key to Baran's room from the old man and look around for anything he might have left behind and that included my camera. He'd made it plain that he didn't want to be caught with what, in his possession, would be contraband. The chance was the slimmest, but as long as it was there I had to look.

We walked to the end of the hall and started down the stairs, the creaks that would have warned me of Baran's coming loud. The old man was at his counter, his back to us. He turned his head at the sound and I saw recognition and surprise leap vying into his eyes. He started to reach for something under his counter.

Something whirred past me and the old man yelped and grabbed at his reaching arm. I saw the blood start from between his clawing fingers. Kort had fired at him with his crossbow.

I made the rest of the stairs leaping. I went under the counter for whatever it was the old man had been going for and came up with a heavy spacer's gun. Gas fired, powerful, it flung a slug to rip a man's protective suit open to the vacuum of space and a wrenching death. In an atmosphere, the slug flattened on impact and tore a hole large enough to take out a man's guts. A lethal weapon and a despised one.

I rammed it against the old man's bony side. "Hello," I said. "And how are you, too."

He cringed away from me, he tried to. "I'm bleeding," he said as though he didn't believe it.

I believed it. Kort's flechette had gone through his upper arm and come out the other side. Now its pencil length was sticking up at an angle from the wood top of his counter. The vanes that were meant to steady its flight had cut a cross going through and the old man was bleeding. But blood has an interesting quality. A little often looks like a lot.

"Yes, old man, you are. You'd better do something about it before you pass out from the loss."

He mumbled something I did not catch and moved away. He tried to. His weapon I was holding in his side went with him. "Hey," I said. "Where are you going?"

"I'm bleeding. I got to get it stopped."

"Of course. You must, before you pass out. But tell me, why did you want to shoot me?"

"I . . . I didn't know it was you. You . . . you startled me."

"Right. You always go for your gun when you hear a guest on the stairs behind you. It's a reflex action."

"That's it. It was a reflex action. Let me go. My arm, look how I'm bleeding."

"A reflex action. You thought I was dead and got scared when you saw I wasn't and went for your gun."

I was guessing, but suddenly I was sure I knew why Baran would come to this hole of a rooming house in an abandoned service town when he could have more easily stayed at the measurably better spacepad hostel.

The old man was rolling his eyes, oily yellow globes in a face gone bloodless. The gun in his side had to be hurting him, but with his arm he didn't seem to be feeling it.

"Listen," I said. My voice sounded very reasonable, at least to my ears it did. "You're going to bleed to death right here if you don't do something about that arm."

I heard a pounding on the outside door. The eatery had been empty when the old man went for his gun. Now someone wanted in. Kort had gone around me, locked the street door and pulled down the stained and ratty shades. A very good man. I said the words aloud, even if he didn't understand me.

"Let me go fix my arm," the old man pleaded. "I feel weak."

He had a good grip on his arm, the bleeding was letting up, but it was well that he thought different. "You ready to listen to a question?" I said.

"Sure, only let me go. I'm gonna pass out."

"Where's Baran?" I said.

"Baran? He's the fat guy checked in same time you did. I don't know. He's gone."

I prodded him with his gun. "You'd better sit down." I said. "On the floor. You pass out standing up, you're going to hurt your head when you fall."

I laughed. "Although I don't see that it matters much if you don't wake up to feel it."

"My arm, please. I don't know any Baran. He came and he went. I don't know where he went." He was starting to babble.

"When you saw me on those stairs, you looked like you were seeing a ghost. Only Baran and Claire Morgan knew they set me out to freeze. I figure it was Baran passed the happy news on to you."

"All right. Baran. It was Baran told me. He ain't coming back. My arm, please."

"Where is he?"

"I don't know. My arm."

He sagged against the counter. A pale old man who was sure he was going to die. If I didn't get him to spill soon, he'd catch on that he wasn't about to. Whoever'd been banging on the door had decided to look elsewhere for whatever it was he hoped to get from the old man.

I put my hand on the land line communicator set to one side of the counter. "I rip this out, old man, there's no way you can get help even if you do come to for a moment after you pass out. Now, one last time, where is Baran?"

"Ach!" the old man gasped. "He will kill me, I know he will."

"That's only a maybe," I said. "Right now you're bleeding for sure."

It helps, sometimes, if the other person thinks you know more than you do. "Don't worry about Baran," I added. "I know about the matrix miner."

The puzzlement I saw in the old man's eyes was genuine. "What . . . what matrix miner?" he said.

I shook my head. "That's some partner you're putting your life on the line for. He doesn't even trust you enough to tell you what you're really into, does he?"

The old man looked at his arm, then he looked at me. He was thinking. I helped him. I jabbed him with his gun.

"I got a number I can call he don't show here a few days," he yelped.

I shoved his communicator toward him. I didn't ease the pressure of his gun. "Call it. Tell Baran you've got a problem and to get here as fast as he can. That's all, then hang up."

I watched his bony finger punching at the communicator buttons and the scar on the top of my head under my flat fur hat started to prickle. I did not recognize the whole of the number, but the prefix was one I knew well enough. It was an official one. The old man was calling the spacepad base.

I watched him talk and then hang up his land line handpiece. The number he'd punched in was not the police aid one and, except for his name up front, he'd said exactly what I told him to say, no more and no less.

"I'm going up to the top of the stairs," I said. "I don't want Baran to see me until he's inside. You stay here and send him up."

"My arm," the old man said.

He kept a small pile of throwaway towels under the counter. I picked up a wad and held it out to him. "Here, press this on it. Baran gets here, you can take care of it then."

With a towel to protect my hand, I worked Kort's flechette free of where it was stuck in the counter, handed it to him.

"Top of the stairs, back in the shadows," I said to the old man. "I can see you, you can't see me."

I motioned Kort to go ahead of me and we went up the stairs. The hunger pangs in my chest would have to wait.

At the top I stopped with my hand on the rail where the old man could see me. One hand. I flourished his gun at him in the other. I wanted him to see that, too. Then I moved back slowly until I figured to be far enough into the dark to turn and run along the wall without him seeing that we were gone.

Along the wall where the floor was the strongest and least likely to betray our movement with its creaking. Into my room and down the line I'd left dangling from the roof's edge in case we'd need a way out, pausing only for our white fur cloaks. I would have liked to kick in Baran's door and search his room for my camera, but I did not think I had the time.

Going out I closed the window all the way and hoped no one would notice it was not locked. I shook the line hook free of the roof, coiled the plaited length hurriedly. I did not take us back up the slope down which we'd come, our tracks in the snow would be too easy to follow. Instead, snatching up our skis, I raced us around to the front of the low building.

Keeping to the traveled part of the street, we made it to the rim of the Heyday dish in time to see spinning red lights tearing along the road from the direction of the base.

I'd been right to heed the scar on my head. The old man had called the base and maybe Baran, but it was police who were responding.

I leaped as far off the road as I could, Kort behind me. Hunched down, in the dark our white cloaks were no more than two more hummocks in the snow.

My plan was uncomplicated. To run *toward* the police. Who goes looking for a fugitive back on the path along which he'd just come?

And then there was that other enemy, *Thul's* killing cold. I did not relish the thought of spending another night burrowed in the snow. I meant to circle back after the searchers had left, go up the line into my room as we had before, and wait out the night in its shelter.

Again, who looks where they have already searched? I might even confront the old man for food. I would know to handle him differently this time.

Four cruisers whipped past us. Two men in each, eight men. A small posse. Red beams spinning out across the snow, washing the sky momentarily as they went over the rim and dipped down into Heyday. Silently, no siren sound to warn their intended quary.

I started to rise, dropped with Kort's warning hand on my arm. One more vehicle. A small skimmer, two seats. No spinning lights, no heads, running dark.

It settled to a stop just short of the Heyday rim. Two men got out, walked to where they could look down at the action below, stood silhouetted against the flashing red glow. I knew them both. Baran and . . . Sten!

Kort was crouched in the snow beside me and it was his partner with whom I'd left Sten. He'd saved me from the old man's spacer gun, but where would he be if I now pointed it at Sten?

I decided not to point it. I put my hand on it under my cloak, flipped off the safety, but did not take it out and point it.

From over the rim the glow burst suddenly white. Bright floods had come on. A bullhorn sounded. Not enough to cover the crunch of the snow under my feet if I tried to come up on Baran and Sten unobserved.

The night wind tugged at me as I stood up, but I hardly noticed it. "Good evening, gentlemen," I called out and enjoyed the start of surprise with which Baran and Sten whirled to face me.

Baran was the first to recover. Almost at once he laughed. A throaty sound. He was fat, but not that fat.

"Pike, you are indeed incredible. My friend Sten has already told me how you survived the inconvenience to which Claire and I put you, and the encounter with that poor man who let himself be pushed into matching his strength against your wits. And now this."

"Inconvenience?" I said. "You wanted to kill me."

"Not really wanted to, Pike. But what else could we do if we were to keep our enterprise confidential? Admit it, Pike, your line of work is not conducive to keeping secrets."

"Where's Meta?" I said to Sten. To see him with Baran was a complete surprise. More than it should have been considering that he'd told me he'd worked on the matrix miner that I'd heard Baran say he'd help set up.

It also brought Sten into a different, sharper focus for me. He no longer looked a court jester with a hunger for his chief's power, nor a man who would save his clan. He now had the color of a henchman, a partner in the search for a tool to plunder the planets.

"Yes, indeed, Sten." Baran said, as if the idea had just occurred to him. "Where is Meta? I assume you briefed her before you left your people."

"I . . . I didn't have time. Not without being seen. I . . . I had to get to you about him."

"No matter, we have him now."

Kort had worked his way around to one side. His eyes were on Sten. He had his crossbow out, but he wasn't pointing it at him. He wasn't pointing it at me either.

I took the chance. I pulled the old man's gun out from under my cloak and jabbed it into the bulge of Baran's stomach hard enough to make him grunt. I owed him at least that much for dumping me in the snow.

"Not really," I said.

Beyond the rim, the bright lights were going out down in Heyday. The police would be coming back this way and my need to meet them was less than overwhelming. That they were there at all told me that a new contingent had been added to those who seemed bent on getting to me. Up to now it had been civilians, powerful civilians, but civilians.

But a local innkeeper had gotten himself bloodied up on my account and that was a matter for official attention. I could have run before by simply making it to the spacepad and shipping off the planet. Now there was no way I could leave. The pad, the only gate off *Thul* was barred to me. I was a fugitive to be arrested the instant I showed up to book passage.

Baran grunted. I poked him again. "Don't be a fool," he wheezed. "I need men, Pike, good men like you. This is big, and getting bigger. Throw in with us."

"Not him," Sten snarled, his unexpected vehemence startling me. He turned to Kort, spat out some words. Kort did not move.

Sten took a step toward him, raised a fist, repeated his words, his voice bristling with command.

Kort said something back to him. Short, low.

Sten went livid. His hand darted behind his back.

He didn't make it any more than the old man had made it. I heard him gagging on Kort's flechette sticking from his throat. Clutching at it with both his hands. In the flashing red light, the blood welling between his fingers looked oddly colorless.

It took him seconds to die in the snow.

I stared down at the sprawled body. I did not need to turn Sten over to see the blade-heavy dagger which he'd tried to snatch and hurl at Kort. I'd seen Uldhaar make much the same motion when he'd reached for his to cut me free of my magician's bonds.

From the look on Baran's face the flechette might just as well have struck him.

The blankness lasted only a moment. His

thick lips set and his eyes narrowed down.
Here was a man quick on his mental feet. The
loss of Sten looked a monstrous one, but he
was already discounting it.

In falling, Sten's flat cap had been knocked
from his head. I picked it up and with it pulled
the flechette from his throat. It was a distinctive piece, not machine crafted, and I saw no
reason to leave it behind to be wondered
over.

I motioned Kort into the skimmer. He re-
trieved our skis, took his bloodied flechette
from my hand and got in. His face was som-
ber and he did not look at Sten's body crum-
pled in the road as he stepped over it. There
had to be more to their exchange than a dis-
obeyed command and a man shooting another for going for his knife. I wondered
toward whom he'd leaned in Sten's struggle
to breach his clan's traditions.

Backing away from Baran, I remembered
his needle gun he'd thrust in my face. He held
it out to me, butt first the way I told him to.
He complied so readily, that I had a bad moment as he did so. I'd met so-called "surren-
der" guns fashioned to fire from the back end
of the barrel to bring down an unsuspecting
would-be captor.

Holding the old man's weapon on Baran, I
slid into the pilot seat of his skimmer. All I'd
wanted from him was my camera and the lo-
cation of the dark patch that he'd spotted on
its screen. The patch that might or might not
be Sten's heat-sucking mining machine that
he said threatened his planet and his people.

Now I had to have more. But with Sten's body in the road and the police cruisers about to crest the rim of Heyday's saucer at any moment, this was not the place to press him for it. I could not risk a physical encounter if I tried to crowd him into the narrow two-seater with Kort and me.

I slammed shut the skimmer's door and lifted off. It would be our shelter for the night. I had a land line number memorized. It had brought Baran to me once, it would again.

Meanwhile, I was now running not only from Baran who wanted me dead to keep his secret, but also from the police.

The police, who would hold me to account for the assault on the old man, and now Sten's killing as well.

There was no way I could know or even guess at what Baran's story to the police would be, but I felt they would have more respect for the deadly cold of *Thul*'s night than to try to track us through it. All the same, I kept the skimmer moving.

At first light I found a broad expanse of ice on which to settle that would not hold the marks of our feet. Under Kort's guidance, I'd taken a wandering course edging closer to his hidden valley. I set the skimmer's guidance system on automatic and sent it off in a direction away from it. It would race across the open places and weave its way around and in the twisted ones until its power pack ran down which, from its gauge marks, would be sooner than I liked.

We went the rest of the way on skis, stopping on high ground to look back along the way we'd come. We saw police vehicles cruising, and I could only hope they were the usual searchers I'd puzzled over and not trackers on our trail.

CHAPTER 12

I sat on my pad and we waited for Meta. My stomach rumbled its complaint and from time to time I caught myself rubbing at my chest, but we could not eat until Uldhaar was through with his questioning.

Kort stood with Rhyf; his report, if that's what it was, had been given in what sounded like no more than a single sentence. Uldhaar's two attendant chiefs were keeping their usual respectful distance.

"Sten's dead."

I said it without preamble when Meta came in with the old woman who'd been sent to summon her and regretted it momentarily when I saw the shock in her eyes.

But only momentarily. Her recovery was as instantaneous as had been Baran's. She gave me a blank stare as though she'd never heard of Sten which, considering the screaming I'd seen go on between them, backed me off a little.

"I've seen Baran," I said. "He asked about you."

"Baran?" she said, as if she'd never heard that name either.

"Short fat guy. Runs with your sister."

"I have no sister."

I'd heard of cultures that denied family relationships, but only in the story tapes. I supposed they could exist outside them and probably did. It would not be the first time one member of a family would not admit to a tie with another.

But Baran's remark to Sten about filling her in before he left linked Meta to him and to Claire no matter what she denied.

Uldhaar shot something at Meta. He sounded like he didn't like us talking to each other on our own. Not at the moment anyway.

His questions which she relayed to me got him no more than what he must already have heard from Kort. The two men had exchanged words, Sten appeared to have gone for his knife, Kort nailed him before he could draw it.

Uldhaar did not look to be broken up over losing Sten. He clapped Kort on the shoulder much as he had me and waved him away. Kort gave a respectful bob and headed for the fire at the center of the hut and the food I smelled roasting there.

Meta started to get up. Uldhaar stopped her. He'd been light with Kort, maybe too light, now his manner sobered. He motioned to Rhyf behind me, and the clansman went to join his mate at his meal by the fire.

Suddenly, Sten's removal from the scene seemed to be making a difference. I could understand that. Uldhaar could now do what he could not risk with Sten contesting him as he had. And if the weapons the shot at me had brought to light were any indication, with enough backing among the chiefs to have brought him down.

Uldhaar's voice was low, Meta interpreting.

Possibly I'd noticed some of his people were missing fingers and ears? I had, at least on the unmittened hand of the hunter who'd tied and brought me in. I did not mention to Uldhaar the two bullyboys in town.

His people knew how to protect themselves from *Thul*'s cold, yet they continued to succumb. It was a new phenomenon and claimed its victims almost before they knew it. He did not wish to alarm his people, but he'd heard rumors of a war machine.

"Tell him about the matrix mining equipment," I said to Meta.

"It's not a war machine. It never was," she said, oddly vehement.

"It absorbs heat. Maybe they walked into a stray emission and didn't know it."

"They'd know it." She sounded as though she had reason to be certain.

I remembered how stricken Baran had

looked when Kort brought down Sten and before he made of his face a mask. I eyed Meta and wondered if the new assurance in her voice had anything to do with her feeling she was now in some way indispensable to Baran.

"Tell him anyway, maybe he already knows more than you think."

She chewed her lower lip over that one before she spoke.

Uldhaar shook his head. He knew of no such device and I could see how he might not. If Sten was working with Baran, he might have tried to convince the chief that a menace existed, but not said what it was. A machine for war could be calculated to move a chief of chiefs more readily than one with which to mine. Maybe it would have if Sten hadn't tried for a power grab, however veiled, at the same time.

"I take it Uldhaar still wants me to find it for him," I said to Meta. "What do you want me to do?"

And when she looked at me, I said, "Don't give me that wild-eyed stare. I heard Baran ask Sten if he filled you in before he left."

She shrugged. "That doesn't mean anything."

"It does if you're the one who has to pass what I say on to Uldhaar. You can tell him anything, and me the same. I want to know whose side you're on."

She let me wonder. I had no choice. Who else was there to interpret for me?

"Tell Uldhaar I think Sten knew more about this machine than he was telling anyone. Tell him I'll find it for him. Tell him if I don't get something to eat soon I'm going to fall over. Tell him."

Uldhaar nodded his understanding. He got to his feet, called his two chiefs to his side. His words to them and to Meta were brief. He kept his eyes on me while she spoke.

He was a true chief. Delegate. Hand the job to somebody who looks like he might be induced to take it on. It's a great idea and has a prominent place in the leadership tapes I had to check out when going up for my rating tests.

A great idea. Except that with Sten gone and Baran alerted to the fact that I wasn't dead, I hadn't the foggiest notion of where to pick up my search. If I went into town or tried for Baran at the base, the police were waiting to pick me up.

And if I failed the charge with which Uldhaar had left me ... well, I'd already seen how these people treated losers.

I rubbed my chest. The recollection did not add to my ease of mind.

Uldhaar left, one of his two attendant chiefs trailing him while the other stayed.

Meta started to follow. "Hold it," I said. "I need you to tell me what's going on."

She gave me her open stare, but she stopped. I walked her over to the old women tending the fire and the food and sat down alongside Rhyf and Kort. I could talk to her while I ate.

"Baran came aboard the same time I did. Maybe you even sent for him, I don't know.

But you had to be here a while before to be as chummy with Sten as you were.

"I can see how Baran might need Sten and you to help him find his machine, but once I located it for him why should it matter to him what happened to Sten? But when Kort's flechette hit Sten, Baran looked like it was him that got it. Why?"

She curled a lip at me. "You don't think all Theodore has to do is walk up to the machine people and say please and they'll hand everything over to him, do you?"

"The clan." I noticed she'd called him Theodore. "He expects a fight and for that he needs men . . . and Sten was his key to getting them. And now there's only you."

She smiled in a way I didn't like. "And you."

"Me?"

She indicated the chief sitting by my pad with her head. "Uldhaar has given orders that you get what you need, that we do as you say." Her smile was tight. "You might have trouble with the clansmen when you order them to attack, but in the end they will do what Uldhaar tells them to do. They will obey you."

"Attack? Me?"

"Why should the machine people be any more generous with you than they would be with Theodore?"

"But fighting men. What does Uldhaar think I mean to do that he expects me to need fighting men?"

"Ask Uldhaar. But don't rely too much on

what he answers. He told you his people are losing fingers and ears. Some are losing more, some are turning up dead. Frozen.''

Dead men and a chief of chiefs who kept his own counsel on what he felt I ought to know. Sten had challenged him and now Sten was gone. I'd given his people reason to regard me as a wizard of sorts and maybe Uldhaar felt that made me a threat to his power as well. Maybe it was the size of the weapon stockpile the search for the needle gun had turned up that had him jumpy. Maybe he was setting me up for a fall as he well may have Sten.

I'd come to *Thul* on the possible trail of a racing beast that could outrun, outswim, and outfly any other. Now a clan chief was expecting me to find and lead a raid against a machine said to be able to plunder a planet of its buried wealth from a distant orbit and, one, it would appear, which might also kill.

Aside from this, I was wanted by the police in a roadside slaying not of my doing, and had no idea who it was that had shot at me with a needle gun and why.

It was this last that concerned me most at the moment. A needle gun is no long-distance weapon. Whoever shot at me had to have been in close, could still be close.

I looked at Meta. A handsome, full-bosomed, well-boned woman whose eyes, brown under the circlet of bangles around her spiked red hair, would be only a little lower than my own. A woman I had no reason to feel I could trust, yet who was the only means I had of communicating with these people other than pointing and gesturing. "How did you get to be here?" I asked her abruptly.

"The clan found me the way they found you."

"I doubt that. You wanted to be found. Why?"

I thought I had the answer, but I was curious as to what hers would be.

She surprised me by laughing. It drew stares from the two old women by the fire and Kort. Rhyf did not look up from the haunch he was gnawing.

"Theodore didn't trust Sten any more than you trust me. He sent me to watch him."

"I don't believe that," I said. "Baran came aboard at the same time I did. You were already here and so was Claire and the old man in town. I think Claire was telling the truth when she said you came here on the trail of breeding stock for your ruined pens. The racing animal story was the one that was out, it brought you here the way it brought me. I think you stumbled on Sten and the mining machine and saw the chance at something that made racing stables look like a cottage industry. You shopped around for an expert in the field and came up with Baran."

"That would make me quite the mastermind, wouldn't it?"

"It would put you at the center of things."

It would also explain why she'd suggested I could take Sten's place in leading a raiding party against the machine should the time come. She knew I wouldn't do it for Baran.

Before she could answer, a young man, taller than the rest of the clansmen, came into the hut and spoke briefly to Rhyf. Meta looked as though she'd heard something she'd rather she hadn't. So did Kort. Rhyf got up and the two left.

I waited for Meta to pass the bad news on to me and when she didn't, I asked her point-blank.

She sighed, "They found two more hunters dead, frozen. This time their animals, too."

"Why send a messenger to tell Rhyf?" I indicated the chief Uldhaar had left behind to see to my needs. "Why not the chief?"

"The chief is a chief, Rhyf is a guard."

I nodded. The chief I could command, but my "helpers" were Uldhaar's security people and, for all I knew, outranked his chiefs in his regard.

"Do you know what I think?" I said to Meta, "I think that Uldhaar isn't the only one not telling me what's going on. I think this mining machine of Sten's is better at killing people than at digging. I think maybe that's why you and Baran want it."

She shrugged. "Think what you like, you're not getting off this planet until you find it. If Uldhaar doesn't see to that, Theodore will."

I don't like anyone to point out the obvious to me, particularly if it sounds like it might be intended as a threat. But finding the matrix machine was not the point for me right now. The point was that I had enough to think about without the need to be looking over my shoulder to see who might be coming up on me with a needle gun at the ready.

I frowned into the hut fire and scraped my brains together. I was no gung ho adventurer and no matter what Meta or anyone thought, I meant to have no part of any frontal assault she and Baran and even Uldhaar seemed to be contemplating once I found the machine, if I found it. A frontal assault was a tactic I always felt was doomed to fail unless you poured in men as though they were fire ants on the advance. And maybe even then.

I remembered that the dark area on my holo camera screen that had caught Baran's attention was fan shaped. I also remembered that Uldhaar had said that his hunters, the ones who came up missing fingers and ears, had been frostbitten before they realized it.

Putting it together, it looked to me like what they would be going against was not a narrowly focused ray, but a spreading field into which they would blunder and be well on the way to being wiped out before they knew they were in it.

I caught myself. I was thinking of the machine as Uldhaar's rumored war weapon and not a matrix miner. But a cryogenic weapon that could freeze a planet from a distance would have any number of advantages. It would disturb the normal patterns of its atmosphere to begin with, creating an instant and devastating ice age. Oceans would freeze. Traffic and transport would come to a halt. Roads, airports, sea-lanes would be

blocked. The distibution of food and energy
and even rudimentary defense would be
made impossible by howling blizzards in
which temperatures plunged to depths never
before experienced outside the laboratory.
And if it were an unsophisticated world, it
could do this without the inhabitants being
any more aware of the reason for the on-
slaught of furious cold holding them in thrall
than Uldhaar's stricken clansmen.

The earth lurched under me. I didn't need the
reminder. If I was to find the machine, I needed
my camera which I hoped Claire still had. I'd
wanted to search Baran's room for it. Now I
knew that it would have been an empty task. If
he was as fearful of being caught with contraband as he gave out, he would hardly have
called in police he could not be sure would not
find it when they turned the hostel inside out
looking for the old man's alleged attackers.

"How do you get in touch with Baran when
you need to?" I asked Meta.

She was steadying herself against the
movements of the earth. "Why should I tell
you anything?" she said.

"Because if you don't, you'll end up with
nothing to hold onto."

My answer seemed to give her pause. "Actually," she finally said, "I don't have a way.
Sten was the go-between. He never told me
how he handled it."

I didn't believe her, of course. But if my seeing Sten with Baran meant anything, he could
have made his contact by doing what I could
in no way do. By simply going in and seeing

the man. As a high panjandrum of the clan he could probably move about without question. Or maybe the weapon-stockpiling chiefs Uldhaar now had under guard covered for him.

"Did Baran or Claire ever get in touch with you?" I asked.

Meta shook her head so that the bangles across her forehead tinkled lightly. "No, we didn't dare risk my being caught. Sten always carried whatever messages there were."

I was no adventurer, but I *was* a journeyman photographer in the midst of a story I meant to have and to break. I saw visions of a wartime experiment gone awry, illicit experiments continued. Even the police cruising in obvious search fit into my mental image.

My sleeve camera had a broad spectrum of sensitivity, but it had neither three-dimensional nor true infrared capability. Without my holo unit I was frustrated.

The bangles circling Meta's hair caught my eye and an idea stirred. I held out my hand to her, swept the circlet from her head when she set her mouth in refusal after I asked her for it. She glared at me, took a flat horn case from the bag at her waist, poked at her disturbed spikes visible in its small mirror.

It was a narrow band braided of stiff filaments that could have been horsehair, except that there were no horses on *Thul*. Dangling from it at close intervals as well as studding it were crescents and circles and lozenge shaped bits of polished stone, some of which had the clear look of quartz.

It was one of these last that I held up to the

fire, then yanked free. Ruby red, it was far from optically clear, but it would have to serve.

I took my record camera from its pocket on my sleeve, held the bit of Meta's bright circlet over the lens and shot the fire. It was wasteful of my power pack to proof the photo at once, but there was no other way.

The image on the narrow plastic strip was dark, but not entirely black. The fire glowed a bright spot at its center, whether by its heat or just light I could not be sure. I would have to wait until dark as I had when searching with my holo camera. But I had no viewing screen to watch. I would have to proof each shot as I made it and hope my power pack would not give out.

Meta'd been watching me, interest sparking her eyes. It would not have surprised me if she knew what I was about.

"Ask Kort," I said to her, "if the messenger who came for Rhyf said where the latest two bodies were found."

But she'd heard the man speak. "Yes, I can take you there."

"Not you," I said. "Kort."

Meta leaned forward, her eyes hard and shining and I remembered her scream that had come to me out of the pressing crowd when it looked as though I was about to be the subject of their clan's champion's tender ministrations.

I remembered and again felt the skin on the back of my neck begin to crawl. "Not you," I repeated. "Kort."

CHAPTER 13

Uldhaar's security men were still on the scene when Kort and I swept up on our skis. A dozen and more loosely spread out across the open snow, Rhyf seeming to be in some sort of charge. From what I could see, all the animals had not gone down at once. One beautiful female in particular caught my attention. She lay as if asleep, a diamond touch of black at the tip of one ear.

I tried to think back to the snowy animal I'd first seen racing up the slope after her playful pup, and felt a little troubled that I could not remember whether she had had such a marking.

I looked about at the surrounding high peaks. Somewhere among them had to be Sten's freezing ray. Baran had said it was mobile, but if, once I'd spotted it for him on my screen, he was willing to leave it unwatched while he and Claire went about dumping me out to freeze, then it was probably mobile only in the sense that a field lab unit is mobile. I would check the ground over now and come back after dark with my red filter and pocket camera.

I reasoned that whoever was operating it had not had the time to spirit it away from its most recent victims; could be training its field on us right now.

I flexed my fingers in my mittens, an unconscious gesture to assure myself that the cold I was feeling was no more than that of *Thul*'s bitter air.

I worked my record camera out of its pocket on my sleeve and made a few exposures. I know there are photographers who burn cassette after cassette and then make a selection. Others know what they want, but take insurance shots.

I don't burn tape and I don't take insurance shots. I see what I see and trust my equipment and the light to capture it for me. I have what I want or I don't. If I don't, the next time I'll know how to do it better.

The systems of my two cameras were not compatible, but I considered the plus of my sleeve one. The 2-D would lend its shots a flat look that might well add to the feel of the story. Give an audience accustomed to three-dimensional projections an extra fillip of the unusual and the primitive. Besides, I had my record camera and didn't have my holo one.

I looked at the pattern in which the bodies were strewn across the snow and took a chance that it was in line with the source of the field that had brought them down. I made a shot along it in both directions. I made a second pair holding Meta's bangle filter over my lens even though it was not yet dark.

I made the shots, but pointing my camera one way while facing in another while I did so. I'd often found it useful when shooting candids to hold my camera up to my eye, but to point its lens to the side at my unsuspecting subject. I did it now as a precaution should there be anyone watching who might be skittish about being photographed and decide to flip on their killer machine while we were here and worry about moving it later.

"Pike. Can you hear me? Pike. Over."

Startled, I snapped my head around, not knowing in which direction to look. I recognized the characteristic flatted quality of the sound and I knew the voice. Baran had me in the focal node of a listening eye.

"I hear you," I said in a low voice. "Over." The listening eyes, I knew, were designed to snap atop a sniperscope to give that killing convenience the added dimension of sound. But like any such pickup, it could easily be made to function in the other direction and in no time the units in the field had a talk button. Jury-rigged at first, then made standard equipment.

Rhyf had turned to look at me when I spoke, but I knew he could not hear Baran. Anyone standing a yard to either side of its narrow line-of-sight band that was no more than an extended echo, would not know it was there.

"Has Meta spoken to you about mustering the men we'll need to take our prize? Over."

For someone who claimed to have no way of getting in touch with Baran, Meta had certainly gotten the news of Uldhaar's new charge to me out fast.

"If you know I can do that, then you know she talked to me. I don't understand why she'd think I would. Maybe you can explain it to me."

"I don't know about Meta's reasons, but mine are the two best. Money and power."

"Sten wanted power and he's dead. If money was that big a thing with me I'd have made it while the making was good. I remember mates in my outfit who came off the starships with para bags so stuffed with credits they were met at padside by an armed escort."

The flatness of the listening ear did not hide the nasty note that came into Baran's voice. "Then let me offer you your own neck as inducement. I didn't identify you for them, but I told the police that one of the two men who killed Sten looked familiar to me. I can always go back and remember that it was because he came aboard *Thul* the same time I did."

"You do that," I said. All these beautiful animals dead and a planet threatened because some greedy son would not drop work on a machine that was better left among the junked war ideas. And I don't react well to threats.

"Let Meta know where you want them to pick me up," I said. "Somewhere where we can talk in comfort and I can fill them in on the rest of your story, including your knowing the whereabouts of what they were sent here to find. I'm sure the prison guard will appreciate you holding out on them with that bit of information almost as much as they'll welcome the chance to clean up their assignment and go home."

The last bit about the matrix machine being what the guards were searching for was a wild shot, but it fit. Weapon or tool, it was an abandoned wartime project that someone had picked up and was making dangerous progress using. With the scars of a devastating peace action still unhealed, you couldn't risk the attention you would call down on yourself and your government by reactivating even a branch of the regular armed forces you were publicly demobilizing to go in and wipe it out. And how would you explain piling peace marshals or policemen onto a supposedly empty iceball of a world if you chose to go that route? Assuming you even had somewhere from which you could draw them without it being noticed and your actions called to account.

But what if you gave out that you were setting up a new prison on a remote planet? You would then naturally need to send in penal guards in sufficient numbers. Recruit them from your returning veterans, your discharged MPs, with clear justification. And it was penal guards I'd seen swarming the pad and its hostel.

The click of Baran's weapon on which his sniperscope was mounted reached me before the whir of its projectile went past my ear. From the sound of it, he'd fired at me with a long-range version of the old man's spacer gun, both weapons meant to breach space armor, both ugly against an unprotected body.

I heard Baran laugh, a humorless sound. "I'll tell them where to bury you, Pike, that's what I'll do. You're not going to the police with your story, you're not going anywhere. Meanwhile you think about what has to be done, but not for too long. Tell Meta when you're ready."

I heard a click and a whir and Baran's voice was gone, his "You're not going anywhere, Pike, not anywhere," remembered.

Something atop the nearest peak seemed to be turning back the sun. Something that moved. Natural objects usually caught a beam and held it, then, as the sun's angle shifted, the brightness slowly faded. This reflection flashed and vanished, then flashed again. Snow glasses on a watcher would do it. So would binoculars.

I motioned to Kort to pick up one of the fallen animals, hold it up. I circled him, pretending to shoot. Motioned him to lift it higher, lower. I nodded, slid my camera setting to maximum telephoto, raised it up to my eye, and looked over his shoulder at the mountain peak.

The watcher was there. Glasses to his eyes in one hand, in the other, pointing skyward, the unmistakable spiraling muzzle of a seargun. White on white, like the hunters behind me, except for the betraying reflection, all but invisible.

I did not linger on him to be certain, not even to be sure it was not Baran. I made my shot and continued moving Kort about. Continued my pretense of shooting when he went back to the others. I saw no point in wasting what power I had left in my camera to deceive a distant watcher.

"Turn around slowly, hand me your camera, then fold your arms over your chest." From behind me and in clear Galactic.

And when I did as I was told, I saw it was Rhyf, pointing a needle gun at my stomach. The gun that couldn't be found during the search of Uldhaar's people because it was on one of the searchers. Guard Rhyf.

I crossed my arms across my chest, one atop the other, meanwhile chewing myself out mentally for not going with my first instinct to watch Rhyf when I felt he'd understood me before Meta repeated my question when I asked if he or Kort knew the way into town.

While I was berating myself, Rhyf held out his hand. I didn't need to ask what else he wanted. I took the old man's spacer weapon out from under my cloak and handed it over and when he put his hand out a second time, I sighed and handed over the needle gun I'd taken from Baran.

Rhyf pressed the delete button on my camera, waited for the whir of the reversing tape to stop. He held it a while longer, running down my power. If he knew enough to do that, he was no primitive clansman.

"A deal, Rhyf," I said. "So far you haven't hit on anybody but me that I know about."

I noticed that he was standing closer to me than I would have been to him if it was I who held the gun. But then I might, if I didn't want the others to see what I was doing.

He'd finished canceling my images. He handed me back my camera. "Walk," he said. "Keep on with your picture taking act if you like, but walk over to that rise."

"Act?" I said, "What do you mean, picture taking act?"

He laughed. "Even the best of cameras makes some noise, yours didn't."

I'd been saving power while hoping to fool a distant watcher, it hadn't occurred to me there might be another close enough to hear.

"What's over the rise?" I said.

"Nothing. Nothing at all. It's a sheer drop to the ice below. When you get to the rise, turn around and put your camera up to your face. You're going to go off the edge backing up for a better shot."

"If I'm going over the edge anyway, how do you propose to make me?"

"Because with the fall, there's always the chance you might survive." He lifted up his weapon to make his point, "This is for sure."

"True," I said. "But you won't have to explain the fall. A needle in my guts, you will."

Standoff, I thought, until he smiled. "Then

I'll just have to hope nobody notices the hole, won't I?"

I flexed my fingers inside my mittens. My arms were folded across my chest. He was standing close. I would drop my left down and out to sweep his weapon hand to one side and away from me. With my right I would lash out under his chin. He might pull the trigger and get me, but it would be in the side and not in the pit of my stomach. Or I might knock his arm aside enough for his shot to miss me altogether.

It was a desperate maneuver and one I would never think of pulling under his gun if I wasn't convinced Rhyf meant for me to be dead anyway.

"Why?" I said. "Why would you want to take me out? You're not with Meta and I don't think Uldhaar wants me dead either, not yet anyway."

Rhyf looked surprised. His eyes opened, staring wide before I saw their whites roll up. His gun hand stopped pointing and he sagged into me. I caught him as he went down.

Kort moved in on us, his crossbow already back over his shoulder. He had Rhyf under the arms opposite me. Kort jerked his head toward the rim of the rise. Raising him high, so that his feet would not leave a dragging trail in the snow, we sent Rhyf's body over the edge he'd meant for me.

Kort didn't wait for the sickening crunch from below I knew was coming, but turned and yelled out in his own tongue. If anyone among the clansmen had seen what had just happened he might say something later, but right now no one was volunteering to speak up.

"I don't suppose you know Galactic, too," I said to Kort. He shook his head, and held up two fingers, thumb and forefinger, close together. A little. A very little.

A line went flying out over the edge and Kort went down it to the ice below. I was sure that when Rhyf's broken body came up, Kort's flechette would no longer be protruding from it.

I picked up my camera from the snow where it had fallen from my fingers while I was catching Rhyf. His needle gun was not in sight. Had its weight carried it below the surface, or was it now hidden under the cloak of one of the clansmen milling about? Not Kort's, he hadn't had the chance. Which one, then?

I looked at the peak atop which I'd caught the sun reflected and wondered if Rhyf's attack had been sparked to protect what he thought I'd seen there. I did not feel that at the moment Meta or Claire or even Baran would want me dead. And if Kort's saving me from Rhyf meant anything, neither did Uldhaar.

But the matrix machine people might well feel differently and Rhyf had come at me on the heels of my having spotted the watcher and fixing the proof of it with my camera. That would tie Rhyf to the machine and it made sense for its people to have had eyes and ears in Uldhaar's camp.

Had the watcher with the binoculars seen what had happened to their man? What hornet's nest activity would the sight stir up now that they knew I had the secret of their hiding place?

I lifted my camera and scanned the peak with my finder, this time not trying to mask my intent. I could well understand any agitation I might see. An attempt to resurrect a wartime experiment, whether it involved a matrix miner or a freezing force field, would touch on too many treaties, brush too many memories still raw, for it to be plea-bargained away.

Figures moving about, white on white, many of them. I saw hands cupped around mouths in what had to be shouts. Pointing in our direction. This was more than discovery, the watcher had had to have seen Rhyf go down.

I tried for a shot, but had barely enough power to move the leader. I stuffed my camera back into its pocket on my sleeve. Maybe I could just tell my story to the networks when I made it out. If I made it out.

Kort was on the ice below with Rhyf's body, a second line going down. Now that I had no working camera, there was little for me to do here and *Thul*'s cold was beginning to knife at me through my cloak. Our ski tracks were plain in the snow. I should have no trouble tracing them back to Uldhaar's valley and my pad beside a warm fire.

I strode along. Rhyf's gun was missing. Was it only a clansman grasping his chance for a modern weapon who'd picked it up?

Or was there among Uldhaar's primitives another Rhyf with added incentive to silence me . . . someone who now had the means?

CHAPTER 14

"Is this a bribe?" I said to Meta. My holo camera and its case were sitting on my pad when I came in with two new guards trailing me, men who'd come running at a blast of the portal keeper's horn. A messenger had also gone out along my back trail. I expected that Kort would be hearing from Uldhaar about letting me wander off loose.

". . . or has Baran lost track of his machine and needs me to locate it for him again?" I said.

My camera seemed unharmed, but checking my case, I found all my cassettes missing.

"Smart," I said. "I can use my screen to find Baran's matrix miner, but I have nothing with which to photograph it when I do."

"You'll get your cassettes after we have our

machine." Meta said, her breathy voice a sound not pleasant to my ear. She'd been poking at the hair across her forehead with her fingers. She snapped shut her small horn mirror case. "Stop complaining, you have your equipment back and you're still alive."

I didn't think she knew about Rhyf, so I said. "You mean Baran could have picked me off at any time? I don't think so."

That seemed to puzzle her. "You don't know that Baran took a couple of shots in my direction?" I said.

"Shot at you? When?" Anger flared in her eyes.

"Ho," I said. "So he's acting on his own, is he?"

"Baran is a brilliant man, but he is a fool."

I noticed that she'd called him Baran and not Theodore and wondered if they'd had a falling out.

"He wasn't serious, he just wanted to get my attention. But I agree, he is a fool if he thinks giving me back my camera and the promise of my cassettes later will send me charging up a mountain out of sheer gratitude."

She gave me a take-it-or-leave-it shrug. "It was Claire who told me where to find it, not Baran."

"I thought you said you didn't know Claire."

"What I said was I didn't have a sister."

"No matter, I'm not about to accommodate either Baran or your sister . . . Claire."

I remembered Baran's land line number,

which I'd seen the old man punch in, had an official prefix. "Baran has connections," I said. "Let him ask his police buddies to do his dirty work for him."

"He's not with the police."

"He got them there fast enough when the old man called."

"They remembered him working on the machine from before and asked him to help out when he came aboard. He jumped at the chance, it put him in the middle of things."

The earth under our feet lurched heavily, lightning snarled and crackled in the distance, swept in overhead. Electrical activity in *Thul*'s atmosphere!

"I don't remember lightning before," I shouted to Meta over the din. "You know the machine, what's happening?"

"I don't know. Theodore was always afraid something would get away from them that they couldn't control."

So was Sten, enough to trigger his ill-fated attempt to seize control from Uldhaar with me as witness to his power.

A wall of the yurt shook free and tumbled outward, an icy blast swept in. The earth stopped moving, the lightning snarled and faded. Silence sat heavy.

Then, a woman's wail. A shout ... and another. The sharp chattering barks of the snow animals. Creaking as other huts collapsed. The rush to get outside and away from tottering walls. Uldhaar striding into the shattered village square. Uldhaar stopping squarely in front of me. He'd charged me with investigating the earthquakes, demanded now, through Meta, that I tell him what I knew of what had happened. Was it Sten's accursed war machine?

Before I could frame an answer, there was a commotion at the portal, the keeper's horn blasting an interruption.

The messenger to Kort returning, his face ashen even at a distance, running down into the square.

"The men," Meta interpreted his gasping words for me, "All dead, all frozen in their tracks he says."

Frozen in their tracks. I remembered the sudden chill that had knifed through my cloak and impelled me to leave the scene on my own. I was the one who the watcher atop the mountain had seen discover them and it was me Rhyf had tried to silence. Had the machine people, reaching out with their killing wave to do what Kort had kept Rhyf from doing, caught him and the others, but not me because I was quietly gone, drawn to a warming fire?

By my lights, Kort had been a good man. I saw no reason for him and the others all to have died because someone wanted me, one man.

"Tell Uldhaar," I said to Meta, "Tell him I think I can lead him to his war machine."

And when she started to protest, "Forget Baran. Do you want the planet to shake itself apart? Tell him."

CHAPTER 15

Looking about the village from its shattered central square, I could see that the damage the heaving earth had done was great, but erratic.

A hut was flattened, but the ones on either side of it appeared untouched. Another flattened section and on either side others left standing. Like the peaks of spreading ripples pushed upward, leaving the spaces in between unharmed.

Uldhaar sat on his drum, his chiefs around him, his guards herding clusters of men into the square. Men bound, some with eyes darting about, others downcast, feet shuffling, some plodding to a halt to stand stoically still. All without cloaks against the icy temperature.

Uldhaar's traitor chiefs in whose fiefs had been found the secret stores of weapons was my surmise. Ringing them, others of his guard, crossbows at the ready.

Behind us a small crescent of guards. Uldhaar had grown protective of his back.

"Don't do it," Meta's voice was urgent in my ear, low. Uldhaar was jealous of our conversing on our own. "Don't lead them to the machine. They will destroy it. Give Baran a chance."

"Baran wanted clansmen from Sten to throw against it, what difference does it make who points them at it?"

"Please, delay them, let me get word to Baran what you're doing."

"I thought you told me you had no way to get in touch with him now that Sten is dead."

I saw her fingers working. "I have a way," she finally said.

In the distance, I heard faintly a sharp cracking boom and the echo of a sliding crash. I though back to how little attention we'd given the booming sounds coming from the mountains below the horizon when I'd been stationed here. The sounds of avalanches and glacial ice cracking with the bitter cold.

"They never meant to kill anyone," Meta said, her voice rising. "It just happened. That was the problem. The cold from the matrix went out in all directions. People walked into it and there was no way to warn them away."

No way without revealing what you were up to, you mean.

"Kort and the others didn't walk into what

killed them by accident. Your machine people turned it on them deliberately."

"They aren't my people. Please. Delay the clansmen. Give me a chance to let Baran know."

I was curious. "There are no land lines here and you don't have a transmitter. How do you propose to get in touch with him?"

She took a long time answering. When she did, I felt stupid for not having thought of it myself. "My mirror. I signal him with my mirror."

"I don't see the point," I said. "What does Baran knowing have to do with what happens in the end? The clansmen rush the place, they rush the place. It's what he wanted Sten to get them to do, isn't it?"

Again Meta seemed to be struggling with herself. "Yes," she finally said. "Yes, that's what he wanted from Sten."

Uldhaar was getting to his feet, slowly. Standing, looking at his traitor chiefs who would have conspired with Sten to depose him of his power. He stood on no dais here, yet somehow he gave an impression of looking down on them from some towering height.

His voice, when he spoke was matter-of-fact. Here was no orator seeking to persuade his audience to see something his way, but a man laying on the line for others what was going to be.

"He is giving them a choice," Meta said. "You have found the war machine that shakes the earth under their feet. They can die the death of traitors in the manner of the clan's custom,"—that they stood stripped of their cloaks in this biting cold gave an inkling of what that custom might be like—"or they can redeem their honor and the honor of their sons by destroying the machine that threatens their valleys."

I saw sagging shoulders straighten, here and there a slumped man suddenly stood erect. Others followed and the movements spread. Uldhaar did not wait for the decision to become unanimous. He signaled to his guards and they began to circulate among the standing men, slashing free their bonds with their daggers. It did not escape me that some of the other guards had not moved from ringing the square nor had they lowered their crossbows. From the sidelong glances of the chiefs, it had not escaped them either.

Meta leaped to her feet, turned. A guard blocked her way and she dropped back down onto her heels. "He must be there. Baran must be there."

She wasn't wringing her hands, but the sound of it was in her voice. I didn't understand her reasoning, but it had to be making sense to her.

For myself, if Baran had stayed after he'd taken his shots at me, he would have seen what was happening and could take it from there himself.

On the other hand, I didn't know the reach of the freezing field. He might be there, lying hidden, but caught and frozen as dead by it as Kort and the others.

Cloaks were being handed out among the freed chiefs. Perhaps not their own, but cloaks, white and warm. Sleds, each pulled by a riding beast and stacked with weapons.

Crossbows, the long two-handed swords favored by these short-armed men, long, hooked spears. These I did not see being passed around. It made sense that they not be given out until they were about to be needed.

"You have to do it." The words burst from Meta with an urgency that startled me. Her fists were clenched and she seemed to be having trouble bringing her eyes to focus on mine. It was plain she was fighting herself to say what she was saying to me. "You have to do it," she repeated. "There is no time for anyone else."

She leaned forward and now her eyes were intense. "The matrix. The matrix is the essential part. They stopped the work when the peace action ended, but they were ready to give it up anyway. You see, the whole thing was nondirectional. On a small lab unit it wasn't too bad—they could wear gloves and such against the cold—but when they went to a full-scale prototype it was another matter. People and things froze before anyone knew what was going on. And it was almost impossible to control. It got so cold that the resistance inside it went down to practically zero and once in the system the current just flowed and flowed until it stopped of itself."

"You mean once they turned it on they couldn't turn it off. Meanwhile, everything in sight froze solid."

"Something like that. Baran said that finally they couldn't get anybody to work on it. That's why he quit."

"So why did he come back when you called him?"

"The matrix. . . ."

"Hold it," I said. Two chiefs had detached themselves from the small group backing Uldhaar and were now standing beside the one he'd already assigned to me. Three chiefs looking at me.

"What's going on?" I said to Meta.

"The matrix. . . ."

"Never mind the matrix. I've got three chiefs and a ring of guards staring at me. What's going on?"

Concerned with getting me to do something only Baran was supposed to be able to do, her attention had apparently not been on Uldhaar. I had to wait until she caught up with the gist of what he was saying.

"Even though they are traitors, they are his clansmen. Before he orders them against the war machine, he wants to be sure you have not allowed yourself to be deceived by what may not be. He is sending his chiefs with you to reconnoiter."

"You mean he thinks I may be lying for reasons of my own and he wants them to check me out."

"Something like that, I imagine. He didn't put it that way."

"Why would I lie?"

"Well, you might be wanting to create confusion during which you could escape."

It was a thought I would keep in mind. Uldhaar was back sitting on his drum.

"Three chiefs, me, and the messenger to

take us back to the spot where he found the bodies. Five men. Five chances to be spotted. Too many. Four, if we skip the messenger and backtrack the ski marks. That's still too many. They'll be watching, remember."

"The matrix," Meta tried to say to me while Uldhaar was mulling that one over. I quieted her with a gesture of my hand. Uldhaar was on his feet taking his two swords from his belt.

"As always," Meta repeated. "The wizard of wizards displays his great wisdom. He is correct."

He was talking to me, but he was talking to be heard by his people. What could it hurt to remind them that I was a magician and they had me on their side?

He laid his two swords side by side on his drum. It seemed a symbolic placing. He took a crossbow and a quiver of bolts from a guard. Surprise was in Meta's voice when she interpreted what he was saying to me and to his people.

"He is going with you, just the two of you. At dusk, when the light is most deceptive."

Dusk, when the light is most deceptive, and lookouts traditionally most alert ... and the deadly cold of Thul's *night is hovering.*

The fallen wall of the long hut was back up and roughly secured with thongs to keep out the cold. What with the guards and the chiefs and Meta, I was accumulating more attendants than Uldhaar himself. So far as I'd been able to see, he had but two chiefs and one of them he'd assigned to me.

I sat by the fire, eating. I was not too happy

with Uldhaar's choice of dusk by which to reconnoiter. The light then would be as poor
for us to see by as for any lookout.

But if I was to go out in *Thul*'s gathering
darkness with him, I did not intend to do so
with my stomach empty.

Meta, kneeling back on her heels beside
me, had been seethingly quiet for a long time.
Now that I knew how she did it, I could understand why she was upset. She wanted to
get out to where she could signal Baran while
there was still a sun to reflect off her mirror.
But each time she attempted to leave, a guard
stood in her way. Either Uldhaar knew what
she was about and had given orders, or he
wanted her close by so he could talk to me
when he was ready without taking the time
for her to be summoned. With Uldhaar, it
could cut either way, or both.

Abruptly, Meta leaned forward, "I have
something to suggest," and when I looked up
at her she held up a hand.

"Hear me out," she said. "You must have
guessed by now that not Baran, not I, not any
of us ever intended to make it off *Thul* with
a whole field installation of anything. No, it
was the matrix we wanted, and that . . ." she
looked back at my pad where my camera case
was sitting, ". . . that could fit into your camera case very nicely."

I didn't believe I was hearing her aright.

"First Baran wanted me to find it," I said.
"Then he and Claire tried to kill me when I
did, and now you're asking me to smuggle it

out for the three of you in my camera case.
There's a word for that kind of gall. . . ."

"Not for the three of us," she smiled, "just
for me."

She was crouching back on her heels. Now
she lowered her head so that she was looking
at me through her long red lashes, ". . . for
us," she added.

I laughed out loud. I like women, I like
women a lot. My work, before the peace action changed it all for me, had me in the midst
of intelligent, achingly beautiful women constantly. But there are times when I wonder
where some of them get their ideas.

At my laugh, Meta's body tensed. Rage
flared in her eyes. Flared and died almost on
the instant.

"Baran would be relieved if he knew you
were dealing him out. So would Claire. They
could stop worrying about how to get at the
matrix and go home."

She leaned back on one elbow, her body the
long, slender, promise-filled body of a female
animal. She was not through with me yet.

"Neither of them has accomplished a thing so
far. You were the one who located the matrix,
you are the one who will be running the risk
when you go to retrieve it. And," she pointed
out, "you are the one who is being shot at."

"Shot at, frozen, it doesn't make any difference. I don't plan to retrieve anything," I
said. "All I was ever aiming for was a story."

I half pointed over my shoulder at my holo
camera. "And with no cassettes, it doesn't
look like I have much chance of getting it."

I went back to my food. "All I want now is off this planet. After I see what I can do about making sure your mining machine friends don't freeze any more good people, accidentally or otherwise."

Meta sat bolt upright. "You wouldn't! You . . . you wouldn't just . . . just destroy everything!"

I didn't need to say anything, she knew my answer. Her eyes grew thoughtful. "What if I could get your cassettes for you?"

"Unless it was your idea to take them out of my case and you already have them, you don't have the time to signal Baran to bring them. Look outside, the sun is almost gone."

"But what if I did get them back for you?"

I shrugged. It was she who'd reminded me how many times I'd come close to being dead since I came aboard *Thul*.

A blast of cold air made me look toward the doorway of the hut. Uldhaar's chief had shoved aside the skin flap and was beckoning to me.

I got to my feet, went to my pad and picked up my camera. Its magazine was empty so I couldn't use it to shoot with, but its top telephoto length was greater than that of my sleeve camera and with its infrared capability, it could be set to see in the dark.

"See me in the morning," I said passing Meta. "If I'm still around." I added when I was sure I was out of earshot.

CHAPTER 16

For two men supposedly going it alone, we were a sizable party. My three chiefs, Uldhaar's remaining one, and two guards to do whatever grunt work turned up and, of course, Uldhaar and me.

I was holding on to my stomach with my mind. There was no way I could post to avoid the rocking-boat gait of the beast I was riding. And if I tried to ease my knuckle-aching grip on the reins, the reptile-looking head would twist back and try for my knee with its fangs, first on one side and then on the other.

My discomfiture seemed to amuse Uldhaar and the chiefs. I couldn't speak of its effect on the guards, they were running on ahead in the semi-gloom, eyes bent on the ski tracks in the snow.

"We're getting close," I said to Uldhaar before I realized that he wouldn't understand me.

I needn't have concerned myself. He was calling out to the guards almost as I spoke.

The two men retraced their steps and when they were close enough, he swung off his beast and tossed his reins to the nearest. The animal reared and lifted the man from his feet, but by this time I'd seen these ill-tempered beasts do that often enough not to be startled at my own doing the same when I followed Uldhaar in dismounting and handing over my reins.

He exchanged words with his men and then waved me on ahead of him. From here on it would be as he'd said, just the two of us. I unarmed except for my sailor's dirk, and Uldhaar with a crossbow and at least the one dagger with which I'd seen him slash my magician's bonds. The guards had surrendered their skis to us.

Stealth and guile, I said to myself, stealth and guile. But I would have felt more comfortable if I'd had at least one of the weapons that had gone over the edge with Rhyf.

We halted when we were at a little distance from the high crag atop which I'd caught the sunlight reflected from the watcher's glasses. The peak was bright with the last rays of the setting sun, while we were in a shadowed cleft. It was a plus for us, I hoped.

I scanned the lookout position with my telephoto viewfinder, but saw no movement.

Up and down the mountainside I went with my finder, but there was nothing but blank snow broken here and there by a projecting rock formation or icy ledge.

I pointed at the mountaintop and shook my head and held out my camera to Uldhaar for him take his look.

He waved it aside and out from under his cloak came a short brass tube which he snapped open to a yard's length. A folding spyglass that looked as though it might better be in a museum.

He went up and down the mountainside more quickly than I had, but it was his country and maybe he knew what to look for.

He closed his glass, put it back under his cloak, pointed me on and up.

I wished I'd thought to ask for a crossbow back at the village. But maybe they wouldn't have let me have one and maybe I was better off without it. It took more practice to make an arrow or bolt go where you wanted it to than it did a bullet.

"Right," I said to Uldhaar and moved on out ahead of him, sinking deeper where the snow was soft. My skis had been meant for a man shorter than I by a foot and more and lighter by half a hundred pounds.

At the foot of the rising peak we stopped again, Uldhaar raking it with his glass. The top still caught the last light of *Thul*'s weak sun, but the ledge from which I'd seen its reflection was already edging into shadow. Whatever small advantage our position in the lesser light might have given us was vanishing rapidly.

We'd come this far upright on our skis and I looked at Uldhaar to see if he intended for us to keep on in this exposed fashion. He put his closed glass back under his cloak and motioned me on again.

But I stood, my senses alert. I wasn't listening for a sound, nor was I looking for a telltale reflection. I was feeling for a chill in my body beyond that of the falling night. The ground under our feet had not moved, but that did not mean that we had not been seen and the killing field that had claimed Kort and the others turned on for us to walk into.

I sensed nothing unusual. I tried to get across to Uldhaar what it was I was doing, pointing up the mountain and shivering. If he picked up on my meaning, he didn't show it, but waved me on.

We went on up, our passage leaving behind a herringbone trail I felt could not be missed even in the deepening dusk, but still there was no movement above us that I could see, no sudden chill striking.

We stopped frequently to listen and for Uldhaar to probe ahead with his glass. And I, alert and straining, for the first signs of deadly cold.

Nothing. Nothing but silence and the darkness deepening. From the boldness with which we made the last of the distance to the ledge I think we both knew what we'd find.

The marks of many feet in the scuffled snow. A glazed streak on the overhang where someone had fired a searbeam. Food containers, some full, some discarded. No matrix installation that, if Meta was correct, would have been too large to be so speedily dismantled and moved. Only a guardpost from which to mount a watch and one now deserted.

Uldhaar swept the empty ledge with a questioning arm. I spread my hands. There was no mistaking that men had been here, the scars of their boots on the snow attested to that. There was also no mistaking that they were not here now.

I looked out across the valley and its crevices filling with shadow, here and there the last of the sky glow throwing back a highlight. Uldhaar took out and raised his spyglass. I knew there were commanders who saw in the dead and the wounded the measure of their own dauntless spirit. White cloak and white fur on white snow were difficult to see but whether Uldhaar was of that gung-ho number or not, I knew he was counting his dead.

When he at last lowered his glass and turned to me, his face was grim. I could not see them spread out below, but I knew they were there, the frozen bodies pointing.

The matrix machine had to be close. In line of sight with the line of lives callously wiped out to keep its secret.

I swung my camera off my shoulder, set its angle wide for a first scanning. I followed the bodies and almost missed Baran's fanning dark spot so quickly did it come into view on my screen. I'd thought to find it high on an opposite mountain, instead, it showed at the edge of a near crevasse.

I went to telephoto for a close-up image. It was Baran's fanning of cold I was sure, but narrower than I remembered it. Perhaps they were learning to focus its beam at will.

I pointed out into the dusk, pointed at the spot on my screen, out into the dusk again. I put an arm across my chest and shivered as if with the cold. I didn't know if Uldhaar grasped my meaning all at once, but he looked at my screen and then lifted up his spyglass to search the dimness opposite.

I saw the long glass steady. He closed it and nodded. His practiced eye had apparently found an indication my untutored one did not pick out.

Our descent down the mountain was a headlong plunge, Uldhaar outdistancing me on my ill-fitted skis readily so that when I did sweep up to his hidden clansmen, one chief was already in the saddle and waiting for me to mount my beast held steady for me by a guard on either side of the rearing head.

Our ride back to the village was a silent racing, Uldhaar and the others dropping out of sight behind us almost at once. I did not envy them their icy vigil. If I had known how to convey my meaning to Uldhaar, I would have suggested he allow himself and his men a contained fire against *Thul*'s brutal night. The matrix men were civilians and I did not think it likely they would have a detection device sophisticated enough to pick up a fire's glow if it was not in open sight.

* * *

We found Meta sitting by the fire much as I'd left her. Either she'd given up trying to get away to signal Baran or the guards had held her where she was.

The chief's words to her were terse. Uldhaar had sent him to bring up the traitor chiefs, my task was to return with his two swords. It was taboo, Meta explained to me in an aside, for a clansman to touch them but I, a wizard, could carry them to him with impunity.

I nodded my appreciation of Uldhaar. Even under pressure, his grasp of the protocols of his power did not waver.

From the torchlit square outside the hut, I heard the chief's hoarse voice raised, an answering shout, tight. Clansmen were gathering, more than just the traitor chiefs from the sound of it.

Uldhaar had sent me for his swords and his chief for his men. There was no mistaking that he meant to lead an assault on those who'd killed his people and he meant to do it tonight.

"Tell me about the matrix," I said to Meta. I had to know how easily the men who killed so willingly to keep its secret could move the heart of their machine.

She answered without hesitation. Another time I might have laughed at how ready she was to betray her partners.

"They found a way to control it. Not with outside shields and dampers the way they'd been trying to before, Baran thinks, but within the molecules of the matrix itself."

I'd noticed earlier that she'd stopped calling him Theodore, so perhaps my guess that they'd had a falling out wasn't far off the mark. It could be that he was showing signs of not wanting to share the fruits of his expertise with someone whose only claim in his eyes was that she happened to stumble onto what was going on.

"Baran thinks?" I said. "Doesn't he know? I heard him say he helped set it up."

"No, Baran got out of the original work and never went back. He heard rumors after he left, but he paid no attention to them. There were always rumors.

"He says that cryogenic labs were constantly working on ways to eliminate resistance to electrical current. Somebody, somewhere, came across a material that could block it selectively. It was the opposite of the superconductivity they were looking for, but it was interesting and he wrote up what he'd observed.

"One of the former matrix people saw the published report and came back to *Thul*, found the equipment they'd abandoned and had enough success with the idea it had sparked to form a syndicate to finance more research."

Harry's rumored racing syndicate covering their real purpose, I thought. For men already inclined to gamble, was it that great a mental leap from racing beast to a matrix machine of awesome potential?

"What does it look like?" I asked Meta. I did not know if I would make it to the matrix itself, but if I did I wanted to be able to recognize it.

"Baran never would say. He claimed he'd left the project early and had no idea what shape the matrix might have developed into. But he must have found out something new because Sten said he was very excited and trying hard not to show it the last time he saw him."

Baran was familiar with the machine. He could have seen something in the dark pattern of its field that the others did not. Or he could have renewed contact with a former colleague now part of its team.

"When did he tell you it could fit into my camera case?"

"Just about then."

"When did he give you my camera?"

"He didn't, exactly."

I stared at Meta. She did not look embarrassed to be changing her story of how she'd come by my holo camera.

"He never had it, I don't think," she said. "It was Claire who took it from you, you know."

"You ... you knew she left me to die? When?"

She brushed my question aside with a wave of her hand; it was irrelevant to her. "Will you carry it out for us?" she wanted to know.

"What makes you think I can take it out when Baran, with his connections, can't?"

"Does Customs search your equipment after you show them your CE license?"

"Often."

"Do they tear it apart?"

"Well, no. They're looking for contraband, more or less."

"So one more piece of electronic gear would be just one more piece of electronic gear."

"You mean it's that simple?"

Meta shook her head slowly. "I don't know, but I don't see that Baran would risk it being confiscated if he didn't think so."

So now I at least knew Baran's matrix could be taken for photo gear. However small, however large, simple or complex.

It promised to be a long night. I signaled to the old woman tending the hut fire for food. "You're all mixed up," I said to Meta. "You think that because I chase stories for what has to look to you like small bucks all you need do is dangle big bucks and I'll trip on my tongue hanging out to do anything for them."

She lowered her head, so that her dark eyes were again looking at me through her lashes, except that now she was scowling.

"Let me explain this to you," I said. "There are other things I could do and for more money, but I am a photographer because I like being a photographer. Tomorrow I might like to do something else and then I will do that. Right now I would rather not be a smuggler."

"Then you will die and it will be an exercise in futility because none of us will then have the matrix."

The old woman fire tender was holding the steaming haunch of some small animal out to me. I took it from her bony fingers and bobbed my head in thanks. She showed me toothless gums in a smile and went back to her fire.

I had no answer for Meta. She might be right about at least a part of what she'd said.

I sank my teeth into the hot meat. The best I could think of to do was hope that she wasn't.

CHAPTER 17

We were many, our breath wreathing our faces in the cold. We were as many and more as had crowded the vaulted ice chamber to judge me when I was bound atop a cold-glazed dais. Clansmen and clanswomen too had tailed the traitor chiefs, whether to watch the spectacle or to join it there was no way for me to know.

I saw drums but no bugles, which did not surprise me. Cold metal was not a thing to press against wet lips in *Thul*'s chill temperatures.

Beside me, Meta crouched, her narrow back to the small rise that deflected the night wind only a little. Her urgency to signal Baran seemed to have abated. But there had still been sun when Uldhaar and I left her for our scouting sortie and, with the chief of chief's eyes not there to see, a clansman guard was only a clansman.

From the shelter of a higher rise behind us, the sounds of the beasts, unsaddled and tethered only by their bridles, came to us against the wind.

To the left of me where I lay on my stomach peering over the rise, ten men had stepped forward in response to Uldhaar's barked command. All selected swords from the sleds of crossbows, swords, and spears brought up from our rear. They had no need for scabbards.

They bowed to Uldhaar as if by ritual, dropped to their stomachs to crest the shallow lip of ice and snow. Each holding his rectangular white shield before him, each waiting until the other was well over before following.

The shadowless light from *Thul*'s horizon to horizon canopy of stars blurred detail, but the overall glow from the sky was as bright as the light of an Earthside moon. Even with their shields and white cloaks I did not think the chiefs had much chance of not being seen. Their cover was meant to hide them from animal prey, not an alert human sentry. I recalled how readily I had spotted the solitary tracker on my trail, whoever he might have been.

Ten men spread out laterally into a thin skirmish line. I watched them easing forward across the flat expanse leading to the crevasse on whose lip Baran's dark fanning be-

gan. A fanning I could see only on the screen
of my holo camera. To my eye the rim of the
broad split looked untenanted.

I followed them past the bodies lying frozen in the snow. I followed them individually
also with the telephoto setting of my sleeve
camera. If I saw any hesitate, it seemed to be
only to get his bearings.

I swung my holo camera forward, from now
on I would watch for a change in the darkness of the fan that might signal that its
deadly matrix was being activated. If I caught
it, perhaps Uldhaar could signal his men to
return in time.

It did not happen that way. The men were
nearing the far edge, the arc of their sweep
narrowing, when my screen flared white,
light-struck from rim to rim with a surge of
heat energy.

I snatched my eyes away, semi-blinded, but
I knew the snarl of sear beams well enough
not to need them to know what had happened.

When I could see clearly again, I peered out
but only to count the blackened patches in
the snow.

Uldhaar did not look to me for an explanation. He sat on his drum, his fingers pulling
at his lower lip. It was plain that he knew the
sound of a searbeam as well as I.

I turned to Meta. "You heard that blasting?
If Baran expected a frontal assault by Sten or
me to yield him up his matrix, you can tell
him it won't work the next time you signal
him."

"But if he does get it, will you take it out?"

I shook my head, but whether it was at her single-mindedness or her optimism I wasn't sure.

Uldhaar was off his drum and surveying the scene over the rise with his long glass. He had his two chiefs by him, now he called up a handful more and passed his spyglass around.

When each had taken his turn with it, he pulled them back and they sat in front of him and drew lines in the snow that made little sense to me, but it was their terrain and I supposed they knew what they were doing. But with all the shaking of heads and wiping away of lines, I wasn't sure that they did.

"What's their problem?" I asked Meta.

"The searbeam weapons," she said. "They don't know how to go against them and Uldhaar doesn't seem willing to try a frontal rush. Not yet, anyway."

I laughed, "Too bad Baran's old buddies didn't set themselves up closer under the mountain. Uldhaar could bury their machine with an avalanche."

Uldhaar's head had snapped around at my laugh. "He wants to know," Meta said, "what it is you are laughing at."

"Tell the great man," I said, "that I am not laughing at anything. I am commiserating in my own way over his problem." I wasn't serious about the avalanche.

She repeated my words and then must have added more. Uldhaar was up off his drum and at the rim of the rise again. When he slid back down, he nodded and hit me on the shoulder.

"He says," Meta repeated, "that he continues to be astounded by the wisdom of the wizard of wizards. The positioning as you point out is not of the best, but it will cost nothing to try."

There was dismay in Meta's voice and her eyes were suddenly hollow with it. I was puzzled until I realized that she hadn't taken me to be serious about the avalanche either; that if the matrix machine was to vanish in an overwhelming rush of ice and snow, its magic matrix would be irrevocably lost to her.

But she had me by the arm and was shaking me and saying, "Stop him. He mustn't. Stop him."

"So you'll lose the matrix," I said. "If you want it that badly, you can always come back and dig it up."

Uldhaar was calling out his commands. In quick order his drummers, four of them, were ranged along the rim of the rise. Mingled with them, massed in ranks behind them, were his traitor chiefs. Some had been given swords as before, but now others had crossbows charged, still others carried long, hooked spears.

We were beyond dangerous searbeam range and now that the matrix killers knew we were here there was small point to keeping hidden. Camp fires had sprung up where the clansmen waited.

Uldhaar raised a hand, dropped it, and the drummers crashed into a pounding beat that was all but lost in the tremendous shout that startled me as it burst from the throats of his people, chiefs and clansmen alike. A shout made visible as their breath hit the icy air.

Meta was still on my arm. "We're in the clear," I reassured her. "The slide won't reach us here."

"You don't understand," she was shouting. "Claire . . . Claire and Baran, they're behind it . . . in the crevasse . . . they'll be buried."

I leaped to my feet, but my shout was as nothing in the overall din. Then, as suddenly as they had begun, the drummers fell silent, the clansmen with them. All staring across the open space over which they'd sent their bellow of unsettling vibration.

Across and at the mountain towering against the starry canopy.

Nothing.

Nothing appeared to be happening and, fleetingly, I wondered if I'd wasted time and energy searching these mountains afoot for fear that the roar of my skimdisk would bring their hanging charge of ice and snow down upon me.

But only fleetingly. Slowly, almost imperceptibly, the mountain backing the crevasse began to move. It and its lesser fellow opposite that held the abandoned lookout post.

It moved and slid and gathered speed, a mass of snow and ice and rock pouring down the mountainside with a growing, crashing roar.

Powdering clouds catching the starlight, rolling and billowing to hang on *Thul*'s thin air. But even as their ghastly curtain swirled, I saw that the matrix fan on my screen was undisturbed. Saved by the deep, open split in the ice behind it that had taken the brunt of the crushing, crashing mass.

The matrix saved, but if Meta was right, Claire and Baran were gone. Mercifully if they had chosen to leave their skimmer at a distance and enter the crevasse on foot.

Beside me, Meta seemed genuinely stricken. She was ready to double-cross her partners, but not to see them killed.

The lookout mountain had also let loose a fall of ice and snow and rock in a sweep to bury the bodies of the clansmen in its path beneath a ridge of ice and snow. A bulwark, if Uldhaar chose to use it as such, to bring his forces closer to the menace I could see only on my screen. I saw no advantage to the move since it would place them well inside the freezing field. Yet he might be tempted to throw his traitor chiefs from it in a sudden short dash to overwhelm. They were, after all, not clansmen who'd held loyal to him, but men who were taking advantage of his offer of a clean way to die.

I had no time to speculate. With a wave of his hand and a guttural shout, Uldhaar sent the forward line of standing chiefs over the rim and out at the deadly fan even as the clouds of snow were still rolling.

Out they plunged to vanish into the curling whiteness, each screaming out his battle yell, a hackle-raising sound, a curdling mix of hysteria and bravado and raw courage. A storied sound often mimicked in the videotapes, but never heard in its true pitch save on a field of battle.

I heard the searbeams start their snarl, blending with the yells, rising, overpowering them. Here and there a last lone cry ended in a strangled gasp.

Uldhaar signaled to his drummers and they beat a ragged retreat tattoo. It was a forlorn sound and no clansman came in over the ridge in answer to it. The traitor chiefs standing in massed ranks stood stolid and silent.

I peered out over my holo camera. In the shadowless skyshine I could make out nothing clearly. A rise in the freshly ruined vista could be a fallen body, could be a snowy hummock.

"Wait," I said, and snaked my way over the rise behind us to my unslung saddle on which my camera case was hung.

From its cover compartment I scooped a handful of the flares that were standard for night shots. Back at the ridge, I screwed together the two sections kept separate so that it could not be set off accidentally. I rammed the thin shaft upright in the snow, snapped the activating lever and turned my back.

"Don't look," I said, and heard Meta repeat what I took to be my warning.

I turned when I heard the pop and saw the light as bright as two of *Thul*'s puny suns wiping out the stars. These were not high-ranging floods, only spot illuminators. In a dozen or fifteen seconds, their short drop would be over.

I could make out nothing that I had not seen before.

I sent up a second flare and heard an exclamation from Uldhaar beside me and saw his arm go up, pointing. I followed its direction and thought I made out a squaring in the snow just short of the crevasse rim.

With the third flare I was sure of it. I was looking at the top of a survival bunker, gun slits hidden under a near-flat overhang. Baran's former cohorts had gone underground to work on their device and set up in one of the abandoned bunkers that dotted *Thul*'s terrain.

From what I remembered of them, this one, like the others, was impregnable to anything Uldhaar might have to throw against it short of a lemming flood of bodies to overrun the slits.

"Tell him not to try it," I said to Meta. "He just saw what will happen to his people." As she was repeating my words to Uldhaar, I felt the ground under our feet stir.

I darted for my camera, but even before I brought it to bear on the bunker top, I knew what I would see. The darkness of the fan shape was deepening, its widening field sucking heat from even the hell-chill cold that was *Thul*'s night.

I heard Uldhaar talking rapidly to his traitor chiefs. Those with crossbows were coming forward.

"Tell him not to try it," I repeated my warning to Meta.

Uldhaar listened, then said. "Thank the

maker of brightness and assure him that I
share his concern for the lives of my clansmen.''

It was not a rebuff, I did not think he meant
it to be.

The earth surged under my feet. A rising
and a falling stronger than the first. The air
crackled briefly with a sound that was not of
the wind's making.

It puzzled me. If the bunker's defenders
meant to counter Uldhaar's avalanche with
an earthquake of their making, they could, in
trying to destroy him, also doom themselves.
I did not see a lust for profit, greed, no matter
how ravenous, how conscienceless, breeding
that kind of suicidal reasoning.

Uldhaar gave a hoarse command and the
front line of crossbowmen surged over the
top of the rise, ran to the bulwark the avalanche had flung across the ruined land-
scape, and launched a cloud of bolts at the
gun slits the light of my flares had revealed.

Searguns snarled in the freezing air, some
clansmen fell, but nearly all made it back.

A second line went up and out and another
cloud of bolts flew at the slits and the men
behind them. Again searguns snarled, again
clansmen fell, and again nearly all came back.

Bunkers, impregnable though their design,
were never entirely so on their own. To ward
off attack, they needed to be manned. Given
time, any could be breached.

A bolt or an arrow, even if only one out of
dozens launched, could slip through a slot too
narrow to admit a man's body and find a mark

inside. Uldhaar's men were many and anxious to die cleanly, those inside the bunker could hardly spare a single one of their number.

It was a simple plan and had Uldhaar the time, one with some narrow chance of succeeding. But the evil fan shape I saw deepening, narrowing, reaching out on my screen told me that the killers in the bunker did not mean Uldhaar to have that time.

I shivered with an unnatural chill. On my screen the fan was all but black so absorptive of heat was it becoming. Streamers of darkness were beginning to swirl about it in the imaged surrounding air. I moved away from watching on the rim of the rise and went to warm myself by one of the clansmen's fires.

I almost lost my footing with a surge of the ground under me, the heaving motion adding to my conviction that the bunker killers were grown inexplicably desperate . . . or was the earthquake not the means by which they meant to bring Uldhaar down, but a risk they were accepting to do so in another way?

The cold, even by the fire I felt it knifing into me through my cloak. My breath, a vapor, was freezing on my beard almost as it left my body. A flicker of the unnatural lightning decided me.

I left the fire and ran for the tethered beasts. I snatched up my camera case, slung it over my shoulder, scooped the lariats from the closest saddles.

I seized the bridle of the nearest mount. I did not have time for a saddle, but leaped onto its bare back and raced into the darkness, the shouts of the startled clansmen assigned to guard the animals fading quickly behind me.

The speed of the beast, startling enough when saddled, without the straps of a cinch to bind its body, was breathtaking. The reptile head was stretched out and no more reaching back for me with its fangs than if I were a stable boy.

Out of sight of the bunker and guided by the glow of Uldhaar's fires against the flickering sky, I spun toward the crevasse and was upon it quickly, pulling up my beast, which did not seem inclined to stop, at its edge.

With numbing fingers I secured a lariat about a sizable chunk of displaced rock and lowered myself down the wall of the split, the other lariats looped over my shoulder, the rest of my flares stuffed into my jumpsuit pockets under my cloak. For once, I left my camera behind.

My foot touched bottom sooner than I'd expected and I left the lariat dangling. If I made it back, I would need it to return to my mount and my equipment.

The lightning flashes coming more heavily now gave more than enough light for me to see that the floor of the crevasse was choked from wall to high wall with fallen rock and ice. The debris of Uldhaar's avalanche had reached far.

Here to one side of the bunker the cold did not seem as penetrating, but the movement of the earth now came more often and I saw a disturbance in the atmosphere that made the stars seem to shift and dance. The crackle and hiss was that of lightning, but the bright-

ness I saw leaping had about it a strange look
of folding in on itself.

At each new tremor the walls of ice on either side of me snapped and cracked and sent
chunks to clatter down in near misses. I
pushed aside the feeling that at any moment
they would close shut on me like the jaws of
some huge animal trap.

Ignoring the ominous cracks I saw streaking
darkly up the walls, I struggled uphill, the slope
of the avalanche bringing me closer to the top
of the split backing the bunker. Soon I could
hear the yells of Uldhaar's clansmen mingling
with the snarl of the searbeams and then I was
pressing against the wall of the bunker itself.

I looked up and the gun slits on this side
were an easy reach above my head. I was seeing not the back of the bunker, but its face.

A face whose means of entry the hurtling
mass of Uldhaar's avalanche had buried up
to slits built too narrow for an attacker to
breach, too narrow for a trapped defender to
crawl out of and escape.

They might have stopped their searbeam
blasting and surrendered once they realized
they were trapped.

But if they knew enough about the clansmen to find a Rhyf to spy on them, they also
knew enough to know what to expect if they
did give up.

Suddenly, the why of the Gotterdamme-
rung actions of the men sealed inside the
bunker was clear to me.

CHAPTER 18

The surging of the earth grew heavier. I sensed a rhythmic pattern forming and re-called Sten's warning of a fatal reverberation peak. I had stumbled with the movements be-fore, now I could hardly hold myself pressed against the bunker wall for their violence. I had the feeling that the very air of *Thul* over my head was crystallizing out with the cold. Super-cold flakes that burned and numbed my face at the same time as they brushed it in falling.

The flashes of oddly infolding lightning were coming closer together, their eerie light now an almost continuous flaring, their crash a growing din until the very fabric of the sky seemed about to be ripped apart.

Holding myself up as best I could against

the rocking of the earth, I slid the coiled lariats off my shoulder. I would not need them to reach the bunker slits so close over my head.

I took the flare parts from my pockets, screwed them together for firing.

About me the walls of the crevasse were beginning to split. A ponderous chunk broke free and fell a double arm's length from me, the sound of its crashing lost in the roar of the wind tugging at me, tugging to snatch the flares from my fingers as I worked.

I dropped one and did not bend to pick it up for fear that if I took the time to search for it, the forces the matrix was loosing would overpower me and I would not finish the task I was surprised to realize I had set for myself.

I forced myself to wait until I could pick out the yells of Uldhaar's crossbowmen making another run at the gun slits and the answering searbeam sounds to signal me that no one's attention was on my side of the bunker.

When I thought I did, I activated the firing levers of my flares and lobbed them one by one as rapidly as I could up and into the gun slits. They were not grenades, but they were incendiaries of a sort.

Bright light poured out of the slits, slashing beams to make visible the crystals in the air, clouds of diamond dust sparkling and swirling.

I heard shouts of surprise and anger and did not wait for more, but plunged down the slope of avalanche debris, slipping and sliding and falling with the surging of the ice and rock-studded mass.

A searbeam brushed the air over my head, a desultory sound, a reflex firing. I did not think anyone was aiming to hit me, could even see me for the smoke beginning to pour from the slits to be almost at once whipped away by the vicious wind.

And then came a muffled roar. The top of the bunker seemed to rise up, then settle itself more firmly. My flares did not have that kind of explosive power, but they'd evidently touched off something inside the bunker that did. Flames poured from the gun slits, licking out into a wind that seemed suddenly to be abating.

I paused for no more than a backward glance. The lightning still flashed enough for me to make out the lariat I'd left dangling from the crevasse rim.

I went up it hand over hand. As I came to the top of my climb I saw movement along the way I'd taken racing to the split.

Clansmen! Two! Mounted! Tracking what marks of my beast's passage the wind had not wiped away, bending into it.

They could be the guards Uldhaar had assigned to stand watch over me bent on making up what had to be a dereliction of their duty. Or the tenders of the beasts who'd shouted after me when I'd made off with one of their charges.

I did not know what retribution Uldhaar or tribal custom would exact for allowing me my escape, but for them, guards or grooms, to have come this far through the matrix-generated hell storm spoke to me of determination if not of desperation.

I'd meant to retrieve the lariat I was climbing, but now I did not take the time. Keeping low, I slung my camera case over my shoulder, lifted myself up onto my animal, grateful that it stood quietly for me to swing myself onto its bare back as it never would have if it had been saddled.

With great caution, I guided its head around until it pointed away from my trackers, hoping to be away before they looked up from their task for a lightning flash to reveal me to them.

I didn't make it.

A shout reached me on the dying wind and I did not need to look over my shoulder to know I'd been seen.

I urged my beast forward with my knees. I did not mean to be taken back to Uldhaar and his people. No matter how honored my position as wizard might be, I did not intend to be held captive for no better reason than his wish to keep from the outside world the simple fact of their existence.

A crossbow bolt whirred past me. Not close, the wind was too great for careful aiming, but it meant my pursuers would bring me down rather than allow me to escape them.

I made a hasty reappraisal. Perhaps my station would not be one of as much honor as I'd supposed.

I knew how men traditionally treated horse thieves on my home planet, and I had no reason to suppose that the beast under me, while no horse, would be any the less precious to the clansmen.

I remembered, too, that I was still on sufferance for trapping a snow animal. With the menace of the earthquakes gone, who knew what twisted turn Uldhaar's reasoning would take? And this time, whatever his motives might have then been, there would be no Sten to divert Uldhaar from his choice of fates for me.

Until I heard the bolt whir past me, I'd been more or less attempting to guide my beast. Now I hunkered down against its thick pelt, wrapped my arms around the serpentine neck and gave the animal its head. It snorted in what, in a horse, might have been a neigh, and leveled itself closer to the ground.

The loose skin along its sides that normally would have been confined by a cinch strap tight around its girth, with the wind of its passage flared out to wrap itself over my legs. If I thought the speed of the animal breathtaking before, now it was dazzling.

Crossbow bolts flew past me, closer, their marksmen's aim improving and it may have been that that was making my pulse race, but not entirely.

The rocking-boat gait of the beast I rode was gone, smoothed by its dizzying pace to an easy undulation. Its breath streamed in unlabored puffs of vapor past my head. The animal seemed to be enjoying itself and, in a strange and exhilarating way, so was I.

Ahead! Rising up from the ground beneath

our feet, we on top of it even as I saw it, a bend in the crevasse that put its wide depth squarely across our path.

Late! Too late for me to do anything but brace myself for the expected plunge over its high rim. My beast blind and not even attempting to swerve from the certain doom below.

Not swerving, but not blind.

We hit the rim and went out over it, under me the beast spreading its legs wide as I had seen the falling snow animal do, as Earthside flying squirrels did, as even tree frogs did to catch the air through which they sailed.

On either side of me the loose pelt rose, billowing outward. It was a large animal and the air of *Thul* was thin and we landed heavily.

Heavily but easily and we raced on without so much as a stumble or a break in stride.

In a heavier, more supportive atmosphere of another world, the beast's flight could well be more a soaring than the heady fall cushioned by the parachute effect of its ballooning pelt that I'd just experienced.

This *was* Harry Judd's racing, flying beast I was astride! It had to be, and Baran, in his eagerness to hold on to a bargaining chip, had deprived me of my holo camera's cassettes.

With no charge left in my sleeve camera, I was totally robbed of any chance to record and give proof of its phenomenal prowess.

Over my shoulder I saw my pursuers reining their mounts to a rearing stop, too busy fighting to keep their animals from following the soaring example of mine to send a parting flurry of crossbow bolts after me. But that the setback would be for them only a temporary one, I was sure. They would find another way.

I'd lost track of the time, but the stars overhead seemed to be fading and a jagged outline of peaks was beginning to show against a lightning on the horizon.

It was just as well. The stars of *Thul* were not so familiar to me that I could use them to guide myself, but I did know the relation of my old base and its pads to the rising sun.

I hung the freshening dawn on my shoulder and, except to keep it there, trusted the beast I rode to pick its own way, to know what chasms it could span with its heady, flying leap and which it could not.

When I at last emerged from between the walls of ice and mounds of snow that were the foothills of *Thul*'s mountains, the sun was clearly risen and the pad tower hung low on the distant horizon to guide me the rest of the way.

I found an overhanging ledge above a snowy patch that would take the prints of my mount. I swung up onto it and hoped that when my trackers passed this way intent on the spoor of my beast they would not lift up their eyes to see the marks of my passage above their heads.

My beast did not wait for the shout with which I meant to send it on its way, but wheeled almost as my weight lifted off its shoulders and streaked for the shelter of its home mountains.

I made my way along the ledge a ways before I slid to the ground at its far end. If Baran was true to his word and had not identified me to the police as one of the two men who'd accosted him and Sten, then I didn't think the old man at the hostel would have either.

I settled my camera strap over my shoulder and struck out for the tower. I'd find out soon enough.

Epilogue

The civilian guard guiding the skimmer pulling up to take me out to the launchpad was the same one who'd checked me in. Thickset, his full beard studded with his frozen breath, he eyed my camera case now much as he had then. "Did you get what you came for?"

I ignored the sarcasm edging his voice as I had before. Did I get what I came for?

I'd come to *Thul* in search of an ice beast. I had found it, and I had ridden it. I had also found men and a machine that better deserved to be called by that name.

But my cameras were empty of images and I did not have the piece for which I'd been sure the networks and the syndicates would have clamored.

Uldhaar and his people would vanish into

his hidden valleys. The orientation tapes would continue to show no native population for *Thul*.

The penal guard and his fellows would go on looking for what existed only as a burned-out ruin on the rim of a lost crevasse.

Eventually someone would notice that the earth was no longer shaking and they would abandon their search and leave.

The guard looked to be waiting and I realized he'd spoken to me.

"What?" I said, and he repeated his question. "Did you get what you came for?"

I shifted my gaze past his shoulder, out to the pad and the freighter shuttle poised for takeoff into the cold-bleached sky.

Out beyond it to the far horizon and the craggy mountain peaks out of sight below it but that I knew were there.

Thul's sinus-numbing air knifed at my lungs.

"No," I said, and let it go at that.